No Strings Attached

and other stories

No Strings Attached

and other stories

Howard T. Kleyn

The Pentland Press
Edinburgh – Cambridge – Durham

© Howard T. Kleyn, 1994

First published in 1994
by The Pentland Press Ltd
1 Hutton Close
South Church
Bishop Auckland
Durham

All rights reserved
Unauthorised duplication
contravenes existing laws.

ISBN 1-85821-188-3

Typeset by Carnegie Publishing Ltd, 18 Maynard St, Preston
Printed and bound by Antony Rowe Ltd., Chippenham

Dedicated to my wife, Margaret

Contents

No Strings Attached	1
Crime Watch	14
The Irresistible Force	19
Stamp Duty	24
Arc of Death	29
Poetic Injustice	47
Trial by Conscience	53
R.O. and F.C.	59
Friendly Relations	72
Weather Watch	77
Happy Like Us	82
The Guiding Light	87
Caveat Vendor	99
No Offence Intended	106
The Customer's Not Always Right	114
A Better Proposal	120

Present and Correct	124
The Ferry Game	128
Double Declutch	138
One Measle, One Mump	143
Somebody Else	148
One Step Ahead	153
Command Decision	158
Passing the Test	162
Thanks for the Memory	179
Turning a New Loaf	186
Double Invention	193
On with the New	198
Two's Company	203
Noticeable Errors	208

No Strings Attached

Sir Mortimer Clavering staggered across the elegant drawing-room. One hand clutched stiffly at the hilt of a rapier protruding from his chest. The other, cuffed in velvet and lace, stretched out blindly in front of him. He was obviously dying, but his expression had not changed from its wooden hauteur.

Slowly he sank to his knees – and then rose smoothly and swiftly into the air, vanishing through the ceiling. From somewhere over his point of disappearance a clear young voice rang out.

"Sorry, Bev, I've got his head string caught up on that second lighting batten. I'm afraid he can't die in front of the fireplace, not unless we move the batten."

An older, over-cultured voice answered from out front. "But that was *ravissant*, my dear Caroline! Positively fulminating with suspense! I could almost hear the teeny creak of his bones."

Caroline's flushed face appeared from above, huge and upside down in the miniature drawing-room. "You probably did," she laughed. "I forgot to put the candle grease on his joints."

Her tousled russet hair swept the tiny antimacassars and the dimple in the middle of her chin deepened. "Is it all right if he snuffs it by the sideboard, then? And can I come down, please?"

Beverley Swayne, owner-manager and producer of the Connington Puppet Theatre, sauntered down the fan-shaped auditorium trailing Turkish-scented cigarette smoke. "Yes, yes, *parfait*, my love. Down you come, everybody! Class, dismiss. Off you go . . ."

His thin white hands made shooing gestures as the three manipulators climbed down the steep wooden steps into the wings. He tugged with one finger on a small wire loop and the curtains drew together. Three flicks with the same forefinger and the stage floods and perches were extinguished.

"It's unfolding like a hydrangea bud, my dears, but a little more early Victorian *élan* is still required! Wednesday at seven, don't forget. And I want the whole cast properly hoovered before then; I could see dust on Sir Mortimer's shirt-front and the potboy's apron."

A heaving-on of coats and a chorus of goodbyes cut him short and the little theatre was suddenly dim and silent. Smiling indulgently he locked the proscenium door and turned to leave. A top-hatted head peeped from his coat pocket.

Caroline smiled as she watched him walking down the outside passage towards her, silvery hair swept thickly behind his ears. His polished fingernails stroked his brocaded waistcoat as though about to produce a jewelled snuffbox. As he emerged into the street his knowing, sardonic face crumpled excruciatingly against the sudden sunlight.

"Bev, could I talk to you for a few minutes?" she said. "About that second scene?"

"Nothing would give me greater pleasure, my dear," he murmured. "Are you having more trouble with the parlour-maid when she pushes the trolley in?"

"No, that's all right now. We've brought the thread that moves the trolley up behind the upstage flat so that I can pull it myself when I walk the maid in. No, it's really the lovers' scene that bothers me. I mean the dialogue."

"The dialogue? What's the matter with it, pray?"

"Well, it doesn't always ring true. For instance, the hero says, with quivering hand extended, 'My lady, I seek your permission to speak of the feelings which I entertain for you!'"

"Most *comme il faut* for the period. You think it sounds wrong?"

"Oh, of course it does, Bev. Can't you hear it? It's not the sort of thing a young man says to his girl, in any period – not if he's got any go in him at all, that is. Suppose she replied, 'My permission, sir, is withheld!' that would be the end of that, wouldn't it?"

"Hardly, or the play would come to a premature conclusion!" Swayne chuckled. "But anyway, what would you say is the natural remark in the given circumstances?"

"Well, I can't tell exactly, I'm afraid, but it's not that."

"No? Tell me, what did your young man say to you when he – er – declared himself?" He glanced swiftly at her. "Well, you needn't tell me, but wasn't it something rather similar?"

Caroline coloured slightly and raised her chin. "I haven't – haven't found myself in that position," she remarked.

"You haven't? My, my! Where are the Connington Romeos? This is a situation that must instantly be rectified." He flipped a maroon handkerchief out and laid it on the ground. Dropping one knee onto it he flung out a dramatic hand.

"My dear – my very dear Miss Drewell! Can it have escaped your notice that my regard for you has burgeoned into – into . . ."

"Bev, for Heaven's sake! Do get up. Look, there's someone coming."

"What? Would you spurn me publicly? Are these my just deserts . . . ?"

Desperately Caroline tugged at his sleeve. "Bev, please! They won't understand."

"I fancy most people would understand and approve of the

blossoming of true affection," he twinkled at her, rising and lightly flicking dust from the maroon silk. "I assure you, my dear, that the language of love is full of extravagance – of *bravura.*

"Would you want your ideal beau to say to you, 'Say, Carrie, wanna know what I'm thinking?' as casually as he might say, 'Seen the latest at the Metropole this week?'"

Caroline considered the point. "It might reveal that he was somewhat tongue-tied and therefore sincere," she replied.

"*Mia carissima*! If the lover gets tongue-tied on the stage the resulting silence will reveal not his sincerity but the distant chink of money being returned at the box office."

Caroline laughed. "Bev, you're terrible! You're not trying to understand what I mean."

"I don't have to try, my dear. I understand you only too well. You have somehow gained the kitchen-sink notion that in real life the words of lovers fall into more prosaic cadences than on the stage. But it is not so – as you will discover for yourself, I hope, before very long."

"When I do I'll show you how that scene should go," she said spiritedly. "It needs igniting. I'll make it real – alive!"

"I'll have the set lined with asbestos," said Swayne with mock solemnity.

Caroline made a sound of reproof. "You're laughing at me," she said. "But I meant what I said. See you on Wednesday."

They parted and Caroline turned up Connington High Street in the late afternoon glow, past shopkeepers folding back their awnings and knots of homeward passengers emerging from the station ramp. Her hazel eyes took on a far-away look.

Surely, she mused, it shouldn't be so difficult to bring two marionettes together convincingly on the stage. The Victorian lovers, their faces in shadow, could serve as an abstract picture while their words, in natural speech, came whispering from the dialogue loudspeaker. Possibly a little background music would help – maybe a rose spotlight . . .

"Look out!"

A shriek of brakes hurt her ears and suddenly she was flying backwards through the air to land against an overcoated chest. The iron grip on her wrist relaxed and a pleasant male voice said, "If you really want to inspect the underside of that bus I should wait until it has come to a stop, first."

She looked up and blinked at his clean-cut, smiling face.

"Say 'sorry' nicely to the bus driver," he prompted. Confused, she did so prettily and turned back to him as the double-decker rumbled away.

"I'm so sorry. Really!" she said breathlessly. "I was thinking about something else entirely."

"I rather imagined you were," he grinned.

"You saved my life! How can I thank you?"

He pursed his lips. "I don't truly think you would have been killed," he said consideringly. "Not, as you might say, killed. Just a broken leg, perhaps . . ."

"Well, thanks very much!" she put in.

"However, if you really want to reward me, you might tell me what you were thinking about so deeply that it enabled you to walk across a green light with your eyes shut."

Feeling abashed Caroline explained as well as she could, suppressing Swayne's pavement antics.

"You see," she ended, "what I want to know is the male approach. I mean the ordinary man in love. Does he propose by acting and talking like something out of Sheridan, or . . ." She paused and looked at him speculatively. "That's an idea. *You.* You can tell me."

He made a question mark with his eyebrows.

"Look," she went on, "suppose a young man saved a girl in

danger – like this, just now. You can be the young man. You fall for me on the spot. You know, love at first sight. All right? Well, what would you do next?"

By this time he was looking definitely startled. He cleared his throat. "I – I would probably ask to escort you on your way in case you still felt shock."

Caroline nodded briskly. "Very well, escort me."

"Certainly, ma'am. Er – where were you going?"

"Nowhere in particular," she admitted helplessly. They laughed together and she realised that his hair had fawn glints in it and his eyes were wide-spaced and grey.

"Let's walk, anyway," he said. They set off down the hill, his hand at her elbow gently steering her through the evening crowds. "If I'm supposed to be – um – taken with you," he murmured, "we should know each other's names, I guess. Mine is Robert Carne. Call me Bob."

"Caroline Drewell," she responded. "How do you do?"

He contrived a slight bow in acknowledgement. "Now, let me see," he said, "what's next? Ah, of course!"

He left her side, feeling in his pocket, and was back in a moment with a posy from a kerbside stall. Tiny rosebuds and a forget-me-not nestled in a spray of thalictrum.

"Oh, Bob, it's beautiful! But you shouldn't . . ."

"Indeed I should. We're romantically entangled, don't forget. A very suitable gesture, I feel. A very happy one, too," he added, seeing her throat set off by the tiny bouquet.

"But I didn't mean you to . . ."

"And now," he continued, ignoring her blandly, "we will proceed to a little club, of which I am fortunately a member, there to exercise the body and delight the senses."

He swept her, wide-eyed, along several side roads to the edge of the shopping district of Connington. Suddenly they plunged through a small gate and entered a drab brick building through a reeded glass door.

"Haven't got cold feet?" he grinned down at her.

Nervousness stiffened her back. "Certainly not!" she answered.

"Good," he responded, drawing aside a heavy curtain. "That would be a drawback at this kind of club."

She found herself looking over a barrier at a small but beautifully-proportioned skating rink. Couples in colourful clothes circled the ice while three or four youths in dark suits and scarves executed pirouettes and other figures in the centre. Laughter and an occasional shriek echoed like chimes round the high hollow roof.

"Well, Caroline, can you skate?" Robert asked.

"Not very well, I'm afraid," she said.

"Fine, neither can I. We'll improve together."

After that the evening became more and more of a Cinderella dream. They skated, both forwards and backwards, till they were tired. They tried to dance on the ice and fell every two yards, helpless with giggles. Afterwards they sat by the lake in the park, munching shrimps out of a paper bag. Later there was dinner in a hushed restaurant with pearl candles in sconces and wine like lime honey.

Caroline threw back her head. "It's been wonderful – wonderful, every minute of it," she declared. "And you've been most wonderful of all."

"So you like being in love?" he enquired. "I must say it seems to suit you." He took one of her hands and held it between his own. "Caroline, let's do this again."

"Bob, no. I couldn't ask you . . ."

"But I'm asking you. Of course," he observed quietly to the room at large, "we *should* be seeing each other every day. Infatuated with each other. However, I'll settle for three times a week ..." And to Caroline's grateful bewilderment, three times a week it became.

Together they listened to Borodin symphonies at the Cryers Hall concerts and the lilt of nightingales in Thackett Wood. Together they inspected Woman with Pitcher at the local art gallery and something from outer space at the local cinema. Together, too, they visited the lovely estate of Connington Hall – and Robert proposed.

It was a mellow, summer-scented Sunday. Caroline knelt in the shade of an elm making a kingcup chain and Robert lay facing her, propped on one elbow.

Throughout the weeks of their friendship he had steadfastly maintained the affectionate, self-mocking tone which from the beginning he had pronounced suitable to the supposed situation. Now he drew intricate patterns with a twig on the ground and spoke more carelessly than ever.

"Wonderful thing, sunlight. It shines down through the tiniest irregular gap in the leaves but when it reaches the ground it makes a soft, diffused patch of light. Rather like a happy marriage.

"The little circle of light may enlarge or diminish, may grow bright or dim with the passing clouds, but it is always separate and warm, pure and true to itself." He looked up. "Why don't we make a little circle of sunlight, Carrie?"

Caroline's heart swung abruptly into dotted rhythm and her eyes were burning as she concentrated on the small yellow flowers. Did he mean what she thought he meant?

"A symbol – a promise of lifelong sunshine," he said. A ring fashioned from a twisted grass stem dropped into her lap and she missed his intent expression.

Play your role, she told herself. It's all part of the melodrama. Remember the rules!

"La, sir, I protest – you trample on tradition," she declaimed lightly. "Is it not the moon rather than the sun that lights the way to true romance? Keep vigil by the belvedere upon the hour of midnight and . . . we'll see about it," she ended lamely.

Hastily she threw the completed chain over his head and scrambled to her feet, turning away from him. "It's – it's time to be getting back," she suggested.

Before they reached the lodge gates they were discussing the town as if nothing had happened. She told him that she had lived there three years and did not know of the existence of the little skating club. He remarked that he had been there even longer and wasn't aware that the Puppet Theatre had been started.

"They're marionettes, strictly speaking," Caroline replied, "but we have glove puppets as well, so . . . You must come to our first night – as my guest. After all, it was through the play that we met. It's a sort of musical drama set in the eighteen-sixties. I take the part of Sir Mortimer Clavering, a rich recluse. And the parlour-maid as well."

"How on earth do you manage the two different voices?" he asked.

"Trade secret!" she laughed. "I mustn't tell you any more and spoil it. But you will come, won't you? It's a week tomorrow." So the day ended.

In the event he not only came but took her out for a stiff brandy 'on prescription', as he put it, just beforehand. In the cosy pub round the corner he put his hands warmly round hers on the globular glass.

"Caroline, I – I guess it's no secret how I feel about you. You remember – last Sunday at the Hall? I meant every word, darling. I know I didn't put it very clearly . . . Hey, what's the matter?"

"But you – I – oh no! Weren't you going on with the game? Oh, Bob, what have I done?"

"Caroline, whatever is the matter? Don't look so tragic!"

"But you don't realise! I've got to . . ." She broke off and gulped the drink down, choking. "I must go. See you at the stage door afterwards!"

Robert sat back as she disappeared like a panic-stricken deer. He was perturbed. Twice he had tried to offer his life to this beautiful girl and twice she had reacted as if it were a loaded pistol. Shaking his head he finished his drink and wandered back to the theatre.

When the lights first went down he was captivated. An elegant marionette in faultless tails rose from the tiny orchestra pit, bowed to the audience and turned to conduct the overture. There was even a real fire curtain, covered with advertisements, slowly ascending.

Throughout the first scene the novelty of the diminutive stage and exquisitely miming figures held his attention but soon his worry returned and he sat, eyes focused far away, blind to the action before him.

Suddenly he was roused by a passage that seemed somehow familiar. On stage a young suitor knelt before a flaxen-haired girl, all ribbons and flounces, ensconced on a sofa.

". . . the little circle of light may enlarge or diminish, may grow bright or dim with the passing clouds, but it is always separate and warm, pure and true to itself – a symbol, and a promise of lifelong sunshine."

Robert's cheeks flamed as the words came from the loudspeaker. The audience was rapt. For a moment he had the chilling illusion that he and Caroline were sitting in the romantic elm-shade surrounded by theatregoers all waiting to hear his proposal speech.

The play went on but he was deaf to it. No wonder his flint had struck no answering fire! Bitterness stung him as he realised that he himself had been but a puppet – a prototype for Act II, Scene 3, his simple ring nothing but a stage prop.

But then, he thought, hadn't he asked for it, in truth? He had insisted from the start that he was going to act the part of the infatuated 'chance encounter' lover, as requested – had over-ridden Caroline when she tried to put a stop to it.

Could he complain that his words had been used for exactly what she said they were required for – a natural-sounding proposal? Strict justice seemed to say 'no' – and yet surely she should have realised . . .

Enthusiastic applause broke in on his reverie and he looked up to see the cast bowing stiffly from the waist across the footlights. A miniature bouquet came sailing through the air suspended from a near-invisible thread. The flaxen-haired leading lady caught it and the curtains closed for the last time.

Somehow he made his way out to the street and strolled dejectedly away. Well, he reflected, that was that. Caroline and the play, together. Instructive and not without irony. He kicked an inoffensive stone out of his path.

In the next moment Beverley Swayne broke over him like a garrulous comber. He had a grave-eyed Caroline in tow and was talking ten to the dozen.

"And when the vicar's foot caught under the rug, my dears, I nearly died! I thought for a moment that he and the rug were going to make a flying exit together like something out of the Arabian Nights.

"But Caroline, my pet, the proposal scene was superb! Your re-write was heart-clutching – it brought them to the edge of their seats. Don't tell me that was written from life, as you were so keen on doing. It was too, too *fin de siècle* for this harsh era!"

"Oh, Bev, do be quiet! You always talk too much."

"My dear, as a child my favourite toy was a cheerful shiny

jack-in-the-box. He always played the same game but we loved him. Then one day we grew up and his lid was left shut in the attic. When I went up there years later I opened the box once more but Jack didn't move – his spring had rusted away. You must let me push the lid open now and again or I shall rust away too!"

They came to a stop on the pavement outside the upstairs café where the after-show supper was waiting. Swayne disappeared in a swirl of friends and admirers. Robert and Caroline were left temporarily alone; they turned to each other under the globe porch light.

"Bob, what can I say? It was awful of me but I thought – you see, I thought – and then it was too late to change it just before the show. I'm so sorry! Can you ever forgive me?"

"I was a bit cut up at first, I must admit. It's not everyone who has scenes from his inner life presented at a public performance, however drama-laden they appeared at the time."

"I know, I know!" she wailed. "I can't think why I did it, except that I had this argument with Bev and I was determined to show him . . ."

"And you didn't think I was being serious?"

"Well," she fumbled, "I – I wanted to. I wanted to, very much. But I couldn't be sure. You were always acting like – like . . ."

"The boy who cried 'wolf'," he supplied. He took a deep breath. "Well, anyway, the scene went well, didn't it?"

"Oh, it was wonderful! Everyone said so. It rang true."

"In that case," he went on hesitantly, "how about turning it back into real life? There's even a circle of light handy on the pavement."

Solemnly he handed her into it and stepped in himself. They smiled into each other's eyes and his arms came round her, firm and supportive. She raised her lips to his and surrendered herself to the electric magic of his kiss. Her arms tightened round his neck – and then, disturbingly, something was tapping at her shoulder.

They both looked round. Sir Mortimer Clavering, dapper and deadpan as ever in mid-air, bowed like a summoned apparition. Gently the marionette reached out and brought their hands together. He nodded approvingly over them as they clasped tight.

Caroline's eyes followed Sir Mortimer's strings upwards to Swayne's supple fingers at the first-floor window where the entire theatre staff was cheering.

"We're fated!" Caroline laughed. "But I don't mind my answer being public. Yes, yes, *yes!*"

Crime Watch

THE EVENING darkened swiftly but Pamela was so weary that she didn't have the energy to get up from the settee and switch on the light. The glow from the television set in the corner was sufficient for her to find her coffee cup and rough-cut sandwiches on the tray beside her. A small box of sweets lay within reach; they would do for 'afters'.

That was the trouble with her occupation, she thought. It was hard on the legs and feet. Waitresses and hairdressers had the same problem. She really ought to think about a job where she could sit down most of the time.

The TV news and weather forecast had come and gone; the promise of yet more rain did nothing to lift her spirits. Now a real-life crime programme was on and the personable young man on the screen was describing a theft from a shopkeeper a couple of months back. Pamela paid little heed until a picture of the shop front appeared. Then a sudden thrill of recognition ran through her and she sat up in close attention. She knew that shop well!

The presenter's voice came through to her. "... and a particularly ironic feature of this crime is that Mr Tilger, the owner of the shop, was actually sitting in his office all afternoon while the thief or thieves opened the safe in the stock room and got away with some valuable antiques. Furthermore, his niece was in the shop, serving behind the counter all the time. Here are some pictures of the jewellery and ornaments that were taken."

CRIME WATCH

Pamela leaned forward and peered at the items intently. She recognised some of them; they had been in the shop window from time to time. The presenter turned from the glossy photographs. "Inspector, what sort of information are you looking for in this case?"

A grey-haired man in a white police shirt appeared; he had kindly wrinkles round his eyes. "We are very interested to learn how the intruder managed to break into the safe without making enough noise to disturb the proprietor in his first-floor office or the young lady in the shop itself. Our forensic experts are looking into that right now.

"But that's not all. The contents of the safe were in order at 3 p.m., as confirmed by Mr Tilger's niece. Therefore the thief would have had to open it and get the stuff away from the premises pretty quickly, since the owner left at six o'clock and set the burglar alarm in the usual way. We've verified that. So how did our man accomplish that without being spotted?

"There is no way out to the rear of the premises; the thief would have had to emerge from the front. We feel that no matter how bold and how ingenious he was, somebody in that busy street must have noticed something, even if he slipped past the shop girl. And that's where a member of the public could help us."

The grey-haired man turned to face the camera. "Were you in Handsford High Street on the afternoon of Wednesday, August 18th? Did you walk past Tilger's Antiques? Perhaps you paused to look in the window?

"We want to talk to anyone who was in the area at the time and may have noticed something out of the ordinary, however trivial. If you entered the shop, did you hear any unusual sounds? If you were passing, did you notice a man – or woman – leaving the antiques shop with a bundle under their arm?"

The presenter came into shot again. "If you can help in any

way, please give one of our people a call. Or you may like to contact Handsford Police on this telephone number . . ."

Pamela crossed to the television set and switched it off. She was tingling with excitement. On the afternoon in question she had been in the High Street. Not only that, she had been on the spot, right opposite Tilger's Antiques. It dawned on her that she might have the exact information the police were asking for. Or one item, at least.

She picked up the telephone and called the local police station. She was put through to a detective inspector by the name of Anstey. He answered in what seemed to be a bored, offhand manner. However, when he learned that Pamela didn't have a car he offered to come round right away.

Pamela switched the light on, gathered up the remains of her supper, tidied the sweets away and made some fresh coffee. It wasn't long before a knock at the front door signalled the detective's arrival.

She opened it to find a slim careworn man in a crumpled grey suit. "D.I. Anstey, Handsford Police," he announced casually, flicking an identity card in front of her. "I believe you telephoned us a few minutes ago – about the Tilger's robbery?"

"Good evening," Pamela said pointedly. "Come in. Have a seat – and some coffee. I think I may be able to tell you something of interest."

"Indeed?" Anstey didn't seem impressed by the invitation or grateful for the coffee. Pamela guessed that he had developed his hard-bitten attitude as a defence against garrulous witnesses. He walked into the room, sat down at the table and took out a small black notebook.

"Right, miss, if you'd let me have the details. In your own words," he added, as if she were thinking of giving him someone else's version. His lack of interest was so palpable that she wondered why he had taken the trouble to come round so promptly.

"Well," she began, "I was watching the crime programme on the telly and the man asked people to let the police know if they noticed anything unusual. About the antiques shop, I mean. To be honest I didn't hear any funny sounds. And I didn't see anything actually unusual, like a thief creeping away or anything."

Anstey's look of resignation deepened. "I see," he said. "So what *can* you tell me, miss?"

"Well, the programme said that while the robbery at Tilger's was going on Mr Tilger was right next door in his office. But he wasn't! I know that. He left the shop at about half-past three and didn't return until after six o'clock when Annie Tilger had already gone home."

"Whoa, steady on, miss!" Anstey exclaimed, pencil poised. "Let's take it one step at a time. I gather you know Mr Tilger?"

"Certainly I do," said Pamela. "I work right opposite the antiques shop. I know him well – and his niece too. I tell you he wasn't in his shop that afternoon. I know because I saw him leave and he didn't come back until the evening."

"Is that so?" For the first time Anstey showed a spark of interest. "You saw him leave, eh? That might be crucial, if he faked the robbery for insurance purposes. He would have had to stash the antiques somewhere and of course he had to come back at the end of the day to set the alarm. Was he carrying something when he left, by any chance?"

Pamela concentrated on her memory of events. "Yes, he had a sort of bag, like the ones doctors carry, you know what I mean? He went straight to his car and put it in the boot."

"You're sure of that?" Anstey scribbled a note and then looked up sharply. "Great! This could be the breakthrough we need. You say he didn't return till later in the evening. Now, how do you know that? You couldn't be sure unless you watched the shop continuously for two or three hours."

"But I did do that, in a manner of speaking. I was on the opposite pavement all the time, dealing with my customers. I saw everyone who went in and out of the shop."

Anstey's expression slid from alertness to suspicion. "You did, did you? While you dealt with your – customers? You do realise, miss, that if you tell this story in court the defence lawyer is going to attack your moral character and discredit your evidence?"

Pamela raised her eyebrows steeply. "What do you mean? Why should he do that? I'm a respectable citizen. I've been selling evening newspapers on that corner for three years. That's how I remember that day in particular. It was the one day this year when Mr Tilger was in such a hurry he didn't buy a paper."

The Irresistible Force

It was all my fault, really. If I hadn't had a row with Jill over the rucksacks none of it would have happened.

Jill and I were on a walking holiday in East Anglia, without our boyfriends. We had started out on good terms and spent a few days strolling through the fens, exhilarated by the width of the skies and the mournful cries of the birds.

Then, as sometimes happens on expeditions, some trivial dispute arose about which of us was carrying an unfair amount of weight. It was something to do with tinned food; whether carrying the tins and the opener was justified or whether it was better to carry only a little water and rely on finding a pub for lunch.

The disagreement opened out to include other topics, as these things will. Jill began to question the whole idea of the holiday, especially the featureless countryside.

"But we chose this area so that we wouldn't have to climb steep hills," I reminded her. Jill acknowledged that but grumbled that she hadn't known that we should be trekking across a waterlogged prairie.

"And there's not a soul here!" she wound up. "I bet nothing ever happens here – nothing. If anything exciting happened today I'd – I'd kiss the next copper I met! That's a promise!"

Eventually she had stalked off and I was left at the roadside contemplating an empty landscape. I shouldered my pack and began to trudge forward, wondering if I could have handled the argument more tactfully.

The road ran straight on before me, a large watercourse on one side and fields of vegetables on the other. I knew that I was in Cambridgeshire and that Chatteris was somewhere behind me but that was all. The bird calls were shrill in the wind and nothing moved.

A distant hum from behind me developed into a throb, a rumble and a swish of tyres. A dusty maroon estate car pulled up beside me and the driver grinned out of the window. He was a sharp-faced man of about forty with a quiff of hair over one eye and a Paisley scarf twisted carelessly round his throat.

"Well, now, little lady," he said cheerfully, "you look as though you're in need of a lift. Hop in, I'm going your way!"

Warnings about offers from strangers came back to me from my schooldays. "Thank you, but I don't want a lift," I said as distantly as possible. "I'm hiking, not hitching."

"You'll be hiking all day along Sixteen-Foot Drain," he replied. "Come on, Susan, get in and I'll take you as far as the next village."

I looked up sharply. How could he have known my name? Then I saw Jill's face smirking from the front passenger seat and all was clear. It seemed ungracious to refuse the lift now that my walking partner was already on board, so I climbed into the rear seat with a mutter of thanks.

The car accelerated away and the driver confirmed my guess. "So you had a bit of a spat, you two?" he said. "Well, you'd better shake hands on it. The fens are no place for young women on their own to be wandering about. Your friend told me where to find you. Now, where exactly are you both making for?"

Jill and I looked at each other and laughed. "We don't know," she confessed. "We just took a train to Huntingdon – we thought it must be a nice place 'cos that's where the Prime Minister lives – and started from there. Last night we stayed at Chatteris; I don't know where we separated."

"Well," he said, "this road takes you past Euximoor Fen and across the Old Nene into Norfolk. Upwell is the next village." He pointed ahead. The road stretched away like a ruler and the car was travelling like an express train.

"That'll do us, I expect," said Jill, consulting me with a look of enquiry. "And where are you going?"

The driver squared his shoulders and adopted a dignified expression. "We're opening at King's Lynn tomorrow," he said resonantly. "In the Festival. We come every year; Lady Fermoy, rest her soul, insisted."

"We?" prompted Jill.

"Carrie and me. Double act. Cash and Carrie. I'm Cash – ready Cash, they call me. Always available. Top of the bill at the working men's clubs." He turned his head. "Isn't that right, Carrie?"

A thin squeaky voice answered him from behind the back seat. "That's right, Cash. Cash up and Carrie on, that's the spirit!"

Jill turned a startled face to me. We peered as well as we could over the back of the seat but I could see nothing but a suitcase and a bundle wrapped in a wool rug, with what looked like a clothes line tied round it.

Jill gulped and turned round again. "That was Carrie, I take it," she said neutrally to the windscreen. "Does she always ride in the back like that?"

"Yeah, she never took to seat belts!" Cash said with a sidelong glance at Jill. "No, seriously, she . . ."

At that moment a car with a light on its roof overtook us. A blind in the rear window was raised; on it were two words in large black letters: POLICE – STOP!

Cash sighed and took his foot off the accelerator. The two cars slowed together and came to a stop at the side of the road. On the bank of the watercourse a fisherman dozed under an umbrella and in the sudden silence the police officer's footsteps scratched clearly on the macadam as he walked back to us. I noticed that he was not only young and clean-cut but remarkably good-looking in his uniform.

"Good afternoon, sir," he began. "Practising for Silverstone, are we? Or maybe one of these two is about to give birth, is that it?"

Cash raised a restraining hand. "OK, officer, we were motoring a bit. Dead straight road – no harm done, is there?"

The policeman pursed his lips judicially. "No telling when someone may step out in front of you," he said. "You're putting your family at risk, you know. Would you kindly step out of the car and show me your driving licence, please?"

Cash resignedly got out of the car and reached into his hip pocket for the licence. I leaned forward to Jill.

"Are you daft?" I said. "How did you let him pick you up? He's a weirdo!"

Jill looked remorseful. "Actually, it was I who flagged him down, not the other way round," she said. "I wanted to catch you up. But you're right – he's definitely weird. Hang on – leave it to me!"

She opened the passenger door, got out and went round the back of the car. Unobtrusively she came up to the policeman on the off side, next to my open window.

"We're not family, we're hitchhikers," she whispered to him. "And there's – there's something funny about the car!"

The officer looked at her. "Something funny?" he said. "And what might that be?"

"Well . . ." Jill glanced at me imploringly for support. "There's – someone – in the back. I think. Someone tied up. But she doesn't seem to mind. It's spooky. Her name's Carrie. Have a look; see for yourself."

The policeman hesitated for a moment, tapping the licence on his thumbnail. "Sorry to trouble you, sir, but may we have a look in the back of the car? Just to put the young lady's mind at rest."

Cash didn't seem put out by the request. He calmly walked round to the back of the car and raised the rear door. He pointed to the rug-wrapped bundle and smiled. "You mean that?" he said. "Nothing in there. Only some theatrical props. Things we use in the act."

"That's not true!" Jill protested. "There's someone in there. We heard her!"

As he leaned into the car the thin voice came from the bundle, even squeakier than before. "Help! Help! Let me out! I'm being kidnapped!" it cried. "Don't leave me here to die! Help!"

The startled policeman and Cash reached for the bundle simultaneously. They laid it on the tailboard and Cash unwound the cord, smiling incongruously.

As the folds of the rug fell away a ventriloquist's doll was revealed, with blonde curls and blue eyes fringed with long thick lashes. She had on a cherry-pink dress and a cheap brooch with her name, *Carrie*, in bright lettering.

Cash straightened up and turned to the police officer. "A little jest on my part, officer," he remarked. "No abduction, I'm afraid. Just Cash and Carrie. I suppose you wouldn't give me credit for that? Ha, ha! No credit for Cash and Carrie – get it?"

But I wasn't listening. I was looking at Jill and turning my eyes towards the young policeman, who was still goggling at the doll.

Jill tucked her lips into a secret smile and walked over to him. Shyly she put her arms round his neck.

Stamp Duty

MARTIN HAWKES slouched in his folding chair and stared down the village hall. It was bright and airy, as usual, but none too warm. He was glad of his overcoat.

Around the walls trestle tables were arranged, covered in stamp albums and backed by stands and notice boards with sheets of stamps on them. At the far end he could make out a small dingy stage hung with children's collages, their cheerful colours accentuated by the faded curtains on either side. Some tattered strings of bunting overhead were a reminder of the square dance that had been held the previous weekend.

In the middle of the floor a group of earnest-looking men were conferring together; evidently the judging committee was in one of its *ad hoc* sessions. A number of women – wives and girl friends, no doubt – bustled to and fro with books of raffle tickets and cups of tea. His own wife, Mavis, was there obsessively dusting and tidying, also as usual.

Martin frowned at the busy scene. As the founder of the stamp club he had run evenings like this in the early days, without the aid of a secretary or treasurer or any of the others.

He used to look forward to club events. He enjoyed organising facilities and telling members what was expected of them. They liked it, he knew, and it gave him a glowing sensation. The club was popular and the monthly gatherings soon drew people from all over the district.

Stamp Duty

In fact it had become too popular, he reflected. He had done too good a job. Before long there were covert demands for accountability, then for democratic control and finally for, of all things, respectability.

He was replaced by an elected chairman, his stamp club was rechristened a philatelic society, and the funds were lodged in the local bank. It was all highly dignified and hugely amateur. The glow faded, little by little.

Even so he had continued to serve on the main committee until the election of Mrs Challis as chairman – or 'chair' as she insisted on being known.

Dorothy Challis was an ample woman of ample means. In some regards she was an excellent chair, he couldn't deny it. She was cheerfully tactful, willing to turn her hand to any activity and always ready with a word of encouragement for new or nervous members. Martin acknowledged her ability to get people to work together.

In one respect, however, her appointment irritated him beyond reason. She knew little about stamps – nothing, in fact, compared with his own expertise. However as the widow of an assiduous collector she had a magnificent library of albums from which she could produce displays for all occasions. And that is what she proceeded to do.

With a vivacious imagination which Martin could not but admire, if grudgingly, she persuaded his club (as he always thought of the society) to change direction. There was a move away from lectures on surcharges and overprints or demonstrations of perforating as against rouletting. Themed displays from his own collection were gradually dropped and replaced by other members' exhibits.

To Martin these monthly offerings were of a chilling triviality. There were competitions for assemblies of stamps featuring flowers or inventors or mail planes. Prizes were awarded for the most meticulous arrangement, the prettiest colour combination or the cleverest narrative sequence.

Anybody, however untutored, could win a catalogue or some cash. This evening, the occasion of the AGM, there was even a small silver cup for the best entry on the subject of rail transport!

But the most annoying aspect of all was that Widow Challis seemed to win more prizes than anyone else. She conspicuously excluded herself from the judging committee but the breadth of her inherited collection enabled her to mount displays of all types with comparative ease.

Martin also wondered if she put some of these displays together before announcing what the subject was to be for the following month. In that way, he suspected, she could ensure that her display was of the highest quality.

Attendance at the meetings was higher than ever but the varying formats were not Martin's idea of a stamp club's activities. He was not averse to some lighter topics in philately but surely a club owed a duty to its members, a duty to instruct rather than entertain? If it failed in that duty there was little point in forming a club at all, other than as a sort of stamp bazaar for barter and exchange.

Martin looked forward to quenching the thirst for knowledge that must lurk among the membership. However, he admitted to himself that any such thirst was well concealed. His fellow collectors seemed for the most part to be uninterested in, or unaware of, the fact that their stamps constituted a world history of politics, geography, architecture and human achievement.

How many of them knew, for example, that before 1866 Hanover issued its own stamps denominated in gutegroschen? Did any of them have, as he had, a 1954 fiscal stamp of the Kaghan valley issued by Pakistan with a service overprint, not even mentioned in the catalogue? Did anyone care that the Ukraine had signalled its brief independence after the October revolution by impressing tridents upside down on Russian stamps?

Martin had once put these serious questions to Mavis as she swept and tidied and polished. Her response was not encouraging. "Oh, Martin," she said, "you're getting like an old stamp yourself. A bit unhinged. Unhinged, get it?" She giggled under her breath.

He squirmed. Mavis was more interested in keeping the ornaments straight and the artificial flowers dusted than in educating Martin's cronies in the minutiae of postage history. He had withdrawn to his study to arrange his next exhibit, only to be beaten once more by Dorothy Challis.

This evening he could bear the situation no longer. Once again the Challis table bore a magnificent layout featuring world railways, arranged in parallel lines with imitation stations and signal boxes alongside them. His own gallery of Chilean and South African locomotives augmented with Swiss snow-ploughs paled into obscurity.

Quickly he sent Mavis out to the car for his 1958 Spanish Talgo commemorative; that great express train would add a superb touch but the judges would doubtless be more impressed by the lines and junctions at the other table. Quality was not appreciated.

He glanced again at his rival's entry and noticed that as a nearby door opened and closed the stamps fluttered in the draught. An idea formed in his mind. He would never, of course, interfere with another member's display, but it would be natural to wander past and inspect it. Nobody could object to that.

He rose, allowing his overcoat to fall open, and strolled over to the men's toilet. He washed his hands and allowed a couple of minutes to elapse. A few moments later, on his way back, he strode rapidly down the aisle with an abstracted air, coat flapping.

When he re-seated himself he observed with satisfaction that the lines of Dorothy's railway stamps were no longer perfect. Some of the stamps had twisted in position; others were out of line.

The judging committee would not overlook such details. They would expect a better display from a Challis entry. Dorothy herself, chatting to her guests, had noticed nothing; Martin sat back and hummed to himself.

The silver cup was within his grasp. His comprehensive survey of railway centenaries was superior to anything else in the hall, he was sure of it. This time Dorothy had caught him on home ground.

He looked up to see Mavis returning. She was carrying an envelope of the Spanish stamps, as he had requested, to complete his display. Glancing here and there for any sign of dust or disarray she automatically straightened the rows of Dorothy's stamps as she passed. It was done so casually that no one apart from Martin saw the movement.

"There you are," she said brightly. "Now you'll be on the right lines, won't you?"

Arc of Death

If old Andrew had known that the soft thump on the wall which had woken him up was the sound of a man's skull being crushed he might have investigated a little more quickly. And then again he might not. After all, it would never do for the night watchman of a detector station to get flustered because he had been caught dozing.

It all came to the same thing, though. By the time he had stretched and shuffled across to peer down through the nearest window he saw that a few seconds would have made no difference.

The window gave onto a tiny courtyard beside the great alternator shed and down in the courtyard, huddled next to the wall, was a body. With a cold shock Andrew recognised the fair hair and white coat. It was that lad Tom Harker, the duty engineer, with dark cherry-coloured blood already beginning to puddle under his chest. He was savagely, unmistakably, dead.

The little yard seemed to quiver and vibrate in the smooth white security lighting; Andrew, fearing dizziness, pushed himself upright and looked round. Above and beyond the outer wall the bowl-like antennae and detector arrays stood impersonally against the Northern lights in the Argyll sky and the panther-purr of the power plant was faintly amplified by the brick and concrete below. With a shiver he turned away to telephone the station director.

"What's that you say? Harker dead? Good God! How do you

know?" Marsden's voice sounded querulous over nine miles of wire. "All right, I'll come immediately. Better ring up Dr Hoster right away. Get hold of Thompson as well – he'll have to take the rest of the night shift; and ask Mr Carpenter to come over as soon as he can."

Old Andrew grimaced as he prodded the receiver rest. Carpenter, the station manager, did not like being woken at dead of night even in an emergency and would say so. He did say so. As for Thompson he seemed indifferent; probably thinking less of his fellow engineer's loss than of tonight's overtime rate.

Andrew sighed resignedly. The telephoning finished, he made a note in the night log and moved vaguely towards the car park near the gates. He couldn't do anything for poor Harker, couldn't even enter the courtyard where he was lying. It was part of an inner security zone.

He waited in the chill air, clapping his gloves together gently. Carpenter arrived in his dowdy Vauxhall, bringing the relief, young Thompson, with him. He greeted Andrew but did not seem anxious to enter the station.

At last Dr Hoster drove up and got out with his leather bag. A long grey car appeared, swerved round him and screeched to a halt, a cloud of vapour drifting from the exhaust.

At once the tempo of the night accelerated. Marsden started issuing orders even before he left the driving seat of the grey car. He produced a magnetic card key and strode out of the car park.

Together the group followed the director through Decontamination, Thompson gathering up the night's order board to memorise the codes and Carpenter pausing to check the meter banks. By the time Hoster and the others had caught up with Marsden again he had cleared the zone and tripped the indicators.

They hesitated on the edge of the courtyard before the doctor crossed to Harker's body and knelt. The purring machinery was less audible down here and the yard was cold and still. Old Andrew saw Hoster straighten up and look deliberately at Marsden.

"I'm much afraid, Mr Marsden, that this is more a judicial matter than a medical one."

"Judicial? What do you mean?" Marsden's voice came harshly after the doctor's round tones.

"I mean, sir, that this man has been murdered."

* * *

Marsden handed a cup of coffee across his desk to his visitor and leaned back deeply in his swivel chair.

"Well, inspector, how is your investigation going? Or perhaps I shouldn't ask?"

Inspector Charron sipped carefully. "Och, you can ask right enough," he said mildly. "But if we go on as we're doing at present I shall have as little to tell the Procurator-fiscal after six months as after these six hours."

The station director gazed thoughtfully at this policeman whose detective fame was known far outside his native Argyll.

"I suppose there's no doubt that this is murder, inspector? Dr Hoster wasn't jumping to conclusions, by any chance? Couldn't young Harker have fallen accidentally from a window – say, on the third floor?"

"I'm afraid the wounds are quite inconsistent with that, sir." Charron got up with his coffee cup cradled in his hand and began to pace abstractedly.

"First of all the man's head was crushed, not against the concrete paving but against the wall. Second, there's this terrible wound in the front of the torso – clothes ripped open, ribs crushed and so on. It seems to indicate that he was flung sideways rather than downwards, and with superhuman force."

"Fantastic!" Marsden murmured.

"It is that. But fantastic or no, everything in this world has an explanation. All we have to do is find it."

"That would make an excellent motto for our work here," Marsden remarked. "Even more than for most science."

Charron turned and looked at him. "Mr Marsden, can you tell me something of what that work is? Class A security, I know but..."

"Well, inspector, it's no secret that our job is to detect nuclear explosions, in the air or underground. We form part of the worldwide network of detecting stations set up years and years ago, after the Zurich Conference. That much I'm sure you know already.

"The only secret involved is how we do it. Spectrum analysis, electronic seismography, paraneutics – they all come into it. I can't give you details, I'm afraid; our friends in Libya and the ex-Soviet republics would love to learn them."

"Ay. Perhaps you can tell me where this chap Harker fitted in," Charron suggested.

"Tony Harker is – was – one of our best shift engineers. Very bright. Their job is to maintain and co-ordinate the detection system day and night. In my absence they have access to all parts of the station and are empowered to cope with any situation. Generally they stay inside the inner security zone but of course they're in constant touch with other network stations."

"Quite a responsibility. That means that at night time they are the only people with keys to all the restricted zones, doesn't it?"

"That's right, inspector. The keys are personalised magnetic cards. Their orders are to unlock and re-lock all zone doors as they pass through them."

"Harker's card keys were found on him," mused Charron. "They were checked by his colleague, Thompson, as all in order and we know from your own arrival that the zone doors were properly locked."

"This night watchman of yours, Andrew, apparently saw Harker's body within a few seconds of death occurring and no one was near him. Even if they had been they couldn't have got away through three sets of locked doors, leaving the keys in Harker's pocket."

Marsden grunted in agreement. "By the way," Charron went on, "what was Harker actually doing in that yard? Do you know?"

"No one can say for certain now," replied Marsden, "but there are only two reasons that make any sense. One would be to inspect the emergency alternator in the adjoining shed and the other would be to visit the toilet. There's a staff WC just out of sight at the far end; the nearest after that is in the next zone. Maybe he was taken short."

Charron fluttered his fingers dismissively. "Alternator? Is that the machine hitched up to that single-cylinder diesel with the huge flywheel?" He lifted an eyebrow. "Bit old-fashioned, that. I suppose nobody could have arranged a little 'accident' with that lot?"

"Difficult to see how," Marsden said thoughtfully. "To begin with, the engine isn't normally run at night. You can check that if you like. It's only there to provide emergency cover for a power failure. There was no such failure that night.

"And anyway, even if the alternator were in operation there are no staff who know more about it than Harker and Thompson. They wouldn't be caught out by a malfunction."

Charron sighed. "Not only a lack of data but a complete lack of motive, that's the puzzle. Harker was apparently popular, easy-going and not in financial difficulties. That's right, isn't it? He didn't gamble, take drugs or flirt with those CND types. Intriguing!"

Marsden shrugged and the interview was over. Outside the station director's office Charron found one of his own men consulting a creased memorandum book worriedly. "What is it?" he asked quietly.

"Beg your pardon, sir." The man came quickly to attention. "We've located the murder weapon, sir; a heavy steel bar. It was found behind the alternator shed."

"Prints?" Charron queried.

"Afraid not, sir. Wiped off with an oily rag. We've found the rag!"

"Very helpful," Charron commented, not unkindly.

"The doc's had a look at it, sir, and he says the blow was struck with tremendous force. Not downwards, sir, but upwards! A force of several tons' weight, he says. Upwards! No human could have done it!"

* * *

Over the next three days Charron spent his time on more interviews. Harker's opposite number proved the most interesting.

"Tony was alright, I suppose," said Thompson casually in Charron's office. "*Nil nisi* and all that. But he would never have gone any higher. Only arrived ten months ago and expected to be made assistant director any day! His ambition outweighed his experience, if you know what I mean." He flicked cigarette ash somewhere near the ashtray and gazed negligently at the inspector.

"I take it you two weren't close, then. Any reason that anyone would have wanted him out of the way?"

Thompson's eyes fell. "Can't imagine one," he returned carelessly.

And didn't look as though he'd spend much time trying,

thought Charron grimly as Thompson left, banging the office door behind him.

Was it possible that a young engineer of that type would go as far as murder to stop a rival beating him to promotion? It seemed highly unlikely. And if so would he decry the man's abilities to the investigators? In any case, how could he have arranged an upward force of several tons' weight to catch Harker in the midriff at dead of night?

A sharp double tap at the door announced Dr Hoster's burly presence. "Morning, inspector," Hoster began gravely. "How's the case of the Martian Murderer going? Isn't that what they're calling it in the town?"

"I'll give 'em Martians," growled Charron. "Killed from outer space, eh? I suppose they want me to arrest a wee green man with a pointed head!"

"Quite. All the same, inspector, you must admit that my present news is a little – eerie, shall we say?"

Charron looked up at the doctor's unusually serious tone. "Let's have it," he said wearily. "It can't be any more mysterious than the rest of it."

"I don't know. It's about that steel bar that one of your chaps found in the fatal courtyard." Hoster compressed his lips. "I've been running a few tests on it – superintendent's request. You know something? That bar wasn't the murder weapon after all!"

"What? But you said it was the right size and shape. And what about the blood all over one end of it?"

"It was just that – the blood, I mean – that gave the game away," Hoster said meaningly. "You know that certain structural changes take place in human blood after it leaves the body and starts to clot. Also it can absorb impurities from adjacent materials. Well, from a microscopic study of the deceased's blood I can say that these changes had already begun when the bar came into contact with it."

Charron frowned. "You mean . . .?"

"Just so," Hoster nodded. "The murder was committed – with some other similar weapon – and this bar was deliberately smeared with the dead man's blood afterwards."

"Incredible! How long afterwards, would you say, doctor?"

"Around twenty minutes, I should think. Can't define the interval exactly."

"No, of course." Charron leaned forward and pulled absently at his lower lip. "Anyway, it wouldn't be longer than that, assuming that the watchman, Andrew, got the time right when he heard the – the sound. It wasn't more than twenty minutes before you and the rest of them were on the scene, isn't that so?"

"Right enough. But at least this last development can be explained, unlike the rest of it," Hoster put in. "The murderer didn't want us to find the real weapon. I wonder why. He obviously didn't count on our being able to tell exactly when the blood got onto the bar. I should keep that trick up your sleeve for a bit, if I were you."

Charron nodded. "Good idea. That was a smart bit of work, doc. Thanks."

"I'll let you have a report," Hoster said on the way out. He paused with one hand on the door knob. "By the way, I suppose you've heard that about Harker and Stella Carpenter? More than gossip, it seems."

"The manager's wife? What about her?"

"Appears that Harker used to drop in from time to time and hold her hand when hubby was at work," Hoster said heavily. "Being on shift duty gave him opportunities."

"Interesting! Young Thompson told me that Harker had ambitions and that they weren't exactly buddies. That would make sense."

"Maybe." Hoster made a face. "There's some story about the two of them in the Cavalier's Arms one evening. Too many drinks, tempers up, high words . . ."

"That wasn't mentioned in my interviews. Perhaps it was just a Saturday night tiff?"

"More than that, by all accounts. The landlord knows they were discussing Stella. He took care to mention it when the murder became known. Apparently Carpenter's last words were, 'I'm warning you, Harker, if you come round Stella once more I'll kill you!'"

* * *

The inquest and funeral came and went and Charron concentrated on routine. He dropped in at the Cavalier's Arms to get the landlord's story at first hand. He went over old Andrew's story until he – and old Andrew – knew it by heart. Then he talked to Carpenter again, and an unusually subdued Stella. No clues were forthcoming. It seemed that the Person or Persons Unknown were going to remain so.

Charron went back once again to the detector station armed with a special warrant.

"I'd like to have another look at that courtyard, if I may," he told Marsden on arrival. "I have temporary security clearance. No need to send anybody with me – that is, if the zone is accessible."

It was. Marsden used his own card key to let him in and left him. He stood in the middle of the little yard, pulled a pouch from his pocket and filled his pipe slowly.

For the rest of the day he went over the yard and its surrounds with a single-minded concentration that blotted out everything else. He inspected every inch of the wall against which the unfortunate Harker had died and studied the antennae above it. He toured the fuel store and prowled through the Stroboscopic Lab, both of which gave onto the yard. He looked round the staff toilets at the far end and wandered in and out of the silent alternator shed. Thompson appeared once or twice but left him alone.

It was in the shed, late in the afternoon, that he finally came out of his reverie. He was gazing at a board full of spanners and wrenches next to the starter panel and switch gear. His eyes suddenly re-focused and his teeth came down hard on the stem of the empty pipe.

"Yes!" he muttered. "Yes!" An hour later he was in conference at the police station.

That night he and Dr Hoster were standing once again in the courtyard. A strong, slightly unsteady light shone from one of the ground-floor windows into the bare space, lighting up the door of the alternator shed, glinting on the huge flywheel and throwing the far end of the yard into gloom.

"Well?" Hoster enquired.

Charron sucked his teeth briefly. "What the fiction thriller sleuth always does," he murmured. "A wee reconstruction of the crime, *au* Poirot!"

"Reconstruction? But we don't know yet just how the crime was committed so how can we reconstruct it?"

"Oh, I expect it'll all come together," said Charron vaguely. "Don't ask any more questions, there's a good chap. You've been immensely helpful and now I want you as an unbiased witness. Will you help me?"

"Of course. What do you want me to do?"

"I've arranged for young Thompson and the manager, Carpenter, to be here; you'll find them waiting up in the canteen. Mr Marsden has already unlocked the zone door for us. I want you to bring Thompson to that door and have him walk normally across the yard to the toilet, as if he wanted to visit it. Stay back in the doorway and watch what happens."

"What will happen?" Hoster asked.

"I don't know," said Charron innocently. "After that I want you to get Carpenter and go through the same thing again. Is that clear?"

"As mud. Don't tell me – there's a little green man hidden in the toilet." Charron smiled gently as the doctor strode off.

For some minutes the yard remained cold and empty. The ever-present hum of hidden motors took on a note of menace. A faint patch showed where Harker's blood hadn't been completely cleaned off the concrete.

The door across the yard scraped softly and Thompson stood outlined against the corridor lights. He looked wary and nervous, glancing at Hoster beside him.

After a moment he stepped forward, walking along the side of the alternator shed. As he rounded the corner and came face to face with Charron in the shadows he jumped visibly and a nerve twitched in his cheek.

"What the . . .?" he exclaimed, as Charron reached out and drew him back beside him, putting a finger to his lips. Thompson opened his mouth and closed it again.

Another minute passed silently. The door scraped again and Carpenter came through with Hoster. With scarcely a pause he tramped heavily across the yard past the shed doorway and almost bumped into Charron and Thompson. He stopped.

"What sort of game are you playing, inspector? I . . ."

Charron held up a hand. "Ten out of ten, both of you. Let's continue with the experiment." He raised his voice. "Doc, will you get on the internal phone and ask Mr Marsden to step down here for a moment? Tell him we're at the far end of the courtyard."

When Hoster returned the group was once again in shadow by the corner of the shed. The four waited expectantly.

Marsden came through the door so quietly that he took them by surprise. He glanced round the courtyard inquiringly and then wandered in a puzzled way to the centre.

"Inspector? Inspector Charron? Are you there?" He took a few more steps towards the group and suddenly became aware of them.

"There you are! I couldn't see you from over there. What on earth are you doing?" Marsden's voice radiated genial interest.

"In a moment, Mr Marsden," Charron responded smoothly. "First of all I should be obliged if you'd carry out a wee experiment for us. When you crossed the courtyard just now you didn't come straight down the side as most people might. Would you mind going back to the door and walking down this side of the yard – past the shed doorway?"

Marsden made a small gesture. "Really, inspector, I'm a busy man. I'm sure one of my staff could play the part just as well."

"Still, as you're here now, sir, perhaps you wouldn't mind?" Something in Charron's voice seemed to be nudging Marsden into position.

Marsden looked round and licked his lips. He glanced at the light in the window and the dim opening in the alternator shed. "Is everything set up as it was on the night of the – er – accident?" he enquired.

"Everything, sir," Charron said firmly.

Marsden looked round the group again. He made as if to put another question; then he slowly retreated to a position near Hoster at the zone door. He stood motionless.

"Just walk forward from there, sir!" Charron called.

Marsden's eyes seemed to glitter in the uneven light. He took one step forward, then another; he reached the edge of the shed doorway. He leaned forward slightly, peering desperately hard across it and panting slightly.

Suddenly, in the blink of an eye, he turned and sprinted through the door behind him, brushing Hoster out of the way.

"After him!" cried Charron, as they instinctively charged across the yard after him. Hoster turned and was brought up against the dull steel of the door.

"He's locked it!" he exclaimed. "Quick, Thompson, have you got your card key?"

The scream of a police whistle cut him short. A shout sounded from beyond the wall.

"Never mind, he won't get far," Charron observed. He pulled a torch from his pocket and strolled back past the shed. "I've got some men . . ."

Confused sounds echoed in the yard, covering his voice, and from outside a spotlight swung through the air.

Thompson looked up from manipulating the card key. "There he is!" he yelled. They followed his pointing finger.

High above them Marsden was edging along a parapet at the end of the block. In the next second they saw old Andrew thrust open a window near him and he jerked and slipped, teetering outwards.

More beams of light centred on him, illuminating a horizontal dish antenna like a huge filigree saucer below him. At the last moment he leapt desperately and landed squarely in it.

"Don't be a fool, Marsden! The aerial site is surrounded," Charron shouted. "It's no use, Marsden!"

The brilliantly lit figure made no sound. Painfully it gathered itself from its spread-eagled landing and began to climb the fragile radius rods of the antenna. The thin lattice work creaked and buckled under his clawing weight.

Carpenter drew in his breath audibly. "The accelerator!" he breathed. "He's forgotten. It's just below him. That e.h.t. line . . ."

Charron turned quickly. "What does that mean?" he rapped out.

"It means high tension power," came Thompson's lazy impersonal voice. "It means that if he goes through he'll drop onto about eighty thousand volts."

Hoster shook off his horror and moved forward. "Marsden!" he bellowed through cupped hands. "For God's sake, man, lie still. Don't move! Don't look down, just keep still!"

Marsden apparently heard and realised his danger at last. His frantic scrabbling stopped and he hung motionless for a moment just below the thin tubular rim of the antenna. Then he looked up and saw the rim. He detached one hand and reached for it. The hand fell short by a few inches but the sudden movement strained the bent rods too far.

There was a rasping, ringing sound as his heavy body gradually tore its way through the copper mesh. An unearthly scream came from him as he broke slowly away from the torn mesh and descended through the air.

As he fell towards the wall top the horrified watchers saw his body stop with a jerk and swing. For a fraction of a second it turned though an arc until it met the second invisible cable. An eye-searing flash in violent blue enveloped him and there was a sound like a log splitting in the heat.

As the double report of the circuit breakers died away the police spotlight illuminated the blackened, swaying figure.

* * *

It was after midnight by the time the ambulance had completed its unwelcome task and departed. Charron and the others sat round a plastic-topped table in the deserted canteen and drank scalding tea. Gradually, in response to insistent questions, the inspector began to talk.

"Marsden condemned himself, ye ken, out of his own mouth. Odd little remarks – none of them significant on their own but all adding up to something. I think the first one that caught my attention was about the alternator. He said: 'The engine isn't normally run at night; you can check that if you like.' Here was the station director, who could answer all my questions about his domain authoritatively, yet on this he invites me to check his statement. Why?

"Then there was the remark he made to you, Andrew. When you phoned him he said: 'Harker dead? How do you know?' Now, if you come to think of it, that's hardly a normal question to put first. If you're told about a fatal accident you don't ask you informant how he knows, when he's just told you what he knows. It seemed to me that Marsden was somehow expecting the news. Again, why?

"Then you remember he almost beat everyone else to the scene although he lived some miles away. He must have driven like a fiend. Why this desperation, when he knew that the watchman and the doctor couldn't enter the inner zone until someone arrived with the special keys?

"But this was only suspicion. I wanted to know *why* Harker was killed; after all, he was reasonably popular. You, Thompson, were a bit jealous of his advancement but that was hardly a motive for murder, especially for someone of your tolerant attitude.

"He had been lightly mixed up with your wife, Carpenter, but this again was vastly exaggerated by popular rumour-mongering.

You had no cause to contemplate homicide. But if we didn't find out why, we found out how."

Charron reached into an old cricket bag lying by his feet and heaved a steel bar onto the table. Thompson and Carpenter leaned forward.

"The hand rotor!" Thompson exclaimed.

"Exactly. I saw it on the shed tool board. It fits into the flywheel, doesn't it?"

"That's right," said Thompson. "We use it to turn the diesel over very slowly for checking and adjustment. Was this the – the . . .?"

"Ay, it was that," Charron said levelly. "The scheme was simple in essence. Marsden fixed this bar into its slots in the flywheel when no one was looking, clamped it and started the engine. The sound soon merged with the general hum of machinery. But the bar swung out in a deadly arc through the shed doorway in just the right position to catch anyone walking past."

"But whoever it was would have seen the blurred arc of the swinging bar in his path," objected Hoster.

"Ah! That was the clever part," Charron said. "Marsden took care to fit up the largest stroboscope in the window of the laboratory, shining into the alternator shed. The stroboscope, as you know, has a bright flickering light source which can be set to any given frequency.

"Marsden synchronised it with the flywheel and arranged for the flicker to come when the bar was somewhere inside the shed on each revolution. When it swung outside it was, to all intents and purposes, invisible.

"Andrew said the courtyard seemed to quiver and vibrate as he looked down into it, remember? It wasn't your nerves after all, Andrew."

"Hang on, it might have been any of us!" blurted Thompson, wide-eyed. "How did he know it would be Harker – and on just that night?"

"There was no particular night, I suspect," Charron explained. "He probably set his infernal trap every time Harker was on night duty, banking on the fact that he would pass by eventually. His plan was to come in the following morning and dismantle the bar – or, of course, discover the body and remove the apparatus before the doc and the police arrived.

"Unluckily for him the 'accident' *was* seen, or rather heard (he knew in that case the watchman would ring him first) so he had to come in post-haste to clear up there and then. When you were all struggling through Decontamination he went on.

"A few seconds were sufficient to switch off the strobe, stop the diesel, remove the bar, wipe it and return it to the board. He probably rehearsed it. After the doc here had examined the body he had a further minute or so alone and it was then, I think, that he produced the dummy bar, bloodied it and hid it behind the shed. A decoy.

"So – that's how, but not why. We still have no motive – that is what's made it so extraordinarily difficult from the beginning. Why did he kill?"

"I know what the motive was," said Carpenter quietly. They all swung round on him.

"Go on," said Charron.

"Blackmail. Harker was blackmailing him." Carpenter drew a deep breath. "My wife, Stella – well, she's been a bit silly one way and another. You know, some women get a bit lonely; they try it on a bit and then . . ."

He looked down. "It was Marsden who was paying her attention, not Tony Harker. Tony made a pass but he was too young for her. Marsden thought it would be easy, with me on day work;

but he forgot that people on shifts were also about in the daytime.

"How Tony found out I don't know, but when he did he tried to make some money out of Stella. Well, she doesn't get that much from me because she's not over careful with it so he soon realised that was a dead loss. He must have gone after Marsden instead."

"You never said anything about this before," Charron said sternly.

"No, well, you know how it is. Stella and I are splitting up and I didn't want her mixed up in anything more. In any case I didn't for a moment think that Marsden was a killer. I just thought he was lucky to have the whip taken off his back. If he'd been charged with murder I'd have come forward, of course."

"Looks like we're well rid o' both o' them," came Andrew's voice from the end of the table. "That there contraption was a sight too clever for comfort, if you ask me."

"Ay, he was ingenious in a way but not quick-witted," Charron said. "You know, he never called my bluff. When I got him to walk past that deadly flywheel he panicked.

"All he had to do was pause in front of the lab window for a moment. With the strobe light, which I had set up, obscured, he could have seen that the bar was not fixed up and been able to pass the doorway in confidence. Had he done so we could never have caught him. No evidence, no motive, no proof."

Charron shook his head gently. "I think I'll call it Arc of Death, or the Case of the Undetected Detector," he said.

Poetic Injustice

"Hallo, Tom, great to see you. I saw your name in the New Members list and was delighted. Welcome to the Wanderers' Club. They're a good crowd here and the place is well run. You'll enjoy it, I know.

"What about a quick one before lunch? You've got time, haven't you? Course you have. Waiter – could we have a couple of gin tonics in the ante-room, please? Thanks. Come on, Tom, let's find some comfortable chairs.

"Well, well, long time no see, eh? How long is it since we saw each other? Must be eight years. It was at that reunion at the Dorchester, wasn't it? When poor old 'Patsy' Patterson spilt the soup down himself, remember? Yes, must be eight years. And before that, of course, even longer.

"Do you ever think back to those days in Pakistan? When we were young and gay – and didn't need to think twice before using the word 'gay'? Those were the days! 1953, it was, if you recall. You were with BISN, I seem to remember, and I was attempting to keep the local telegraph station going.

"What a job! Trying to ensure that the telegrams kept flowing along the submarine cables. There was a chain of cables from Karachi via Aden up the Red Sea and along the Mediterranean to Gib before turning north to Lisbon and landing in Cornwall. Today it's all international telephony but in those days the cablegram was the thing if a letter was going to take too long.

"1953 was quite a year. There was the coronation in June and Pinza won the Derby. I remember that because I liked to have a flutter at that time. And before that the Hunt expedition conquered Everest. Remember that? There were ten of them, including Hillary who got to the top with Tenzing, and dozens of Sherpas. Headlines all over the world! Hundreds of telegrams of congratulations came in; we had to put on extra staff.

"You know, Tom, I can tell you a story that involved the Everest expedition. You never knew about it. In fact this story has never been told publicly. It was an extraordinary sequence of events – made quite an impression on me. Mentioning old Patterson just now brought it to mind. Extraordinary, it was.

"It all started when I met Patterson at the Boat Club. He was a young chap then, like all of us, and probably had more money to throw about than was good for him. Some of the young first-time expatriates were like that. Sub-tropical climate, nothing much to do after work and a generous salary to do it with. And servants to boss about.

"We called the servants bearers, if you remember – it was some kind of hangover from the Indian Raj. Pakistan had only been created six years before and we white Colonials still retained some respect, eh?

"Well, anyway, Patterson was in the Club one evening being obstreperous. He liked his *chota peg*. Apparently he called in a slurred voice for whisky *pani*, Scotch and water in other words, the umpteenth, but the wise old head bearer brought him *nimbu pani*, that pleasant lime drink.

"For some reason he went berserk. Called old Mirza all sorts of names and ended up throwing the drink over him. The manager took him away and ticked him off and as Club secretary I had to apologise to Mirza and try to hush the thing up.

"I did suggest to Patterson that he resign from the Club; we had no time for that sort of behaviour. He refused, turned on me and was extremely abusive. It was most unpleasant. However a few days later he got himself appointed assistant to the physiologist who was attached to Hunt's team. I wasn't sorry to see him depart to the Himalayas, I can tell you.

"But that wasn't the last of Patterson, unfortunately. About a fortnight later, in May it was, I was listening to the BBC one day just before going home. There was some racing commentary on – as you know, Karachi was several hours ahead of Greenwich time so we got the English races in the early evening.

"Near the end of one race the commentator's voice became frenzied as the favourite, Parsifal, was nearly pipped at the post by an outsider called Whisky Johnnie.

"I wasn't paying much attention until Salim Azhar, the senior operator, knowing of my interest in the horses, brought me a cablegram which had been transferred to us from the inland system. It had been filed in distant Nepal and was addressed to a firm of bookmakers in England. The text read: TWO HUNDRED POUNDS SP WHISKY JOHNNIE WIN ONLY ACCOUNT 53879 and was signed PATTERSON.

"I realised immediately what had happened. Patterson must have been up country at the expedition's base camp and had given his telegram to one of the Sherpas to send off. Obviously it had been delayed while being carried to Kathmandu and had only now arrived in Karachi to be relayed to London. Salim hadn't heard the radio but he had spotted that the bet was too late and came to me for advice.

"I was caught in a dilemma. As you know, all telecoms staff are ethically bound to handle traffic in accordance with the regulations. Something like doctors with their Hippocratic oath. We all sign declarations of secrecy which bind us not to reveal what we may see in telegrams or hear in telephone calls, except on the orders of a magistrate. It is a disciplinary offence to delay any communication, let alone intercept it.

"For a moment I was tempted to confiscate this cablegram, thus preventing the loss of two hundred pounds which was a very considerable sum in those days, and send a message to Patterson informing him. I might even look forward to a reward from him for my initiative. You may be sure that if the telegram was duly forwarded the bookmaker would not reveal its late arrival to his client; he would simply pocket the bet.

"But then darker thoughts intervened. Why should I do a good deed for the obnoxious 'Patsy'? I owed him no favours and he would never know that I had passed up an opportunity to save him a large amount of money.

"Furthermore there was Salim waiting for my decision. Could I blatantly break the rules and hope to retain a position of respect and authority over my staff? What would you have done, old boy?

"Well, to cut a long story short, I told Salim with a somewhat pious air that no cablegram was to be mishandled, no matter what the consequences were to the sender, and that he should send it on in the normal way. Secretly, though, I was torn by guilt. I thought that perhaps I had invoked the letter of the regulations because it was going to mean one in the eye for the repellent Patterson.

"I was still revolving the matter in my mind when I heard the radio commentator's voice again, at the end of the programme. It seemed that Parsifal's jockey had done something reprehensible in the home stretch. After a stewards' enquiry the placings had been reversed and Whisky Johnnie had been declared the winner!

"You can imagine my feelings. Since Patterson's telegram bore a time-of-filing well before the 'off' the bookie would now have to pay out an enormous sum, at the long odds. Had I intercepted the bet, an investigation would have followed and Patterson would probably have been able to claim the equivalent amount from me! I was no lawyer but it seemed to me that he would have a reasonable case.

"I went to the Club that evening in some turmoil. On the one hand I was still ashamed of the fact that I had momentarily yielded to the temptation to intercept the cable. I was even more ashamed that I might have overcome the temptation not by reason of virtue but because someone I disliked was going to suffer.

"Finally I was shocked at the hidden danger of yielding and relief that, for whatever motive, I had not done so. At least I wasn't going to be the patsy in the affair. Pun intended!

"Well, Tom, I told you that the story had never been made public. I couldn't say anything because it would mean revealing the contents of a telegram. End of career in telecoms! But in fact I did tell it to someone later.

"It happened like this. When Patsy got back to Karachi after the Everest triumph he naturally trumpeted his success at the races and even stood drinks all round at the Boat Club. Whisky, of course; I refused mine.

"Not long afterwards I went on leave. As I said I used to have the odd bet now and again; well, it was at a promoter's party at Goodwood that I met Linda, who was some sort of actuary for a London bookmaker. One thing led to another and the following year we married. Lovely girl – you must meet her.

"Well, one day I was telling Linda about Patterson's big win the previous year and the dilemma which still haunted me from time to time. Linda laughed – and went on laughing. I got a bit miffed and asked her what was so funny about it.

"She told me that she knew all about the bet on Whisky

Johnnie. She had been working at Patsy's bookmaker's office when the cablegram arrived. Of course it was too late to lay off such a large bet so when Whisky Johnnie was placed first the bookie had nowhere to go.

"He couldn't pay out such a huge sum and soon afterwards filed for bankruptcy. So poor old Patsy Patterson got neither his winnings nor his original wager.

"What do you think of that, Tom? Unknown to him he lost, then won and finally lost. He never knew, of course. I did think of telling him at that Dorchester do when he spilt the soup but what the hell! That would have been cruel and pointless. I just think of it now as a case of poetic injustice. Cheers!"

Trial by Conscience

"Richard Henry Derwent?"

(A voice. A voice from the evening gloom, starlit, travelling vibrantly beneath the avenue cypresses. A uniform. Smooth creased blue serge suddenly formulated under the pool of light from a torch at the waist. A face, balanced on a column of silver buttons, overshadowed by the familiar helmet, speaking to – him?

Past experience blurred the images of this uniformed voice on the screen of his mind. Imperiously beckoning traffic, shepherding children, trying shop doors at dead of night.)

"... and it is my duty to tell you that anything you say may be taken down and given in ..."

(Nothing to say. The turn of events was predestined. If the chemist's prescription had to be in the car on that last run across the Vale of Evesham then he had to be walking meekly with his captor beneath the cypresses, behind the pool of light caressing the twirling leaves which danced away ahead of them. The dappled brown flooring of light caught at his memory, took him away and back, into the summer, over the hills ...

The dappled brown mud, corrugated by the receding tide, spread away from his feet in shimmering flats, bounded by stone walls and jetties, guardians of the harbour at St Ives. Boats, nets, gulls, easels with their attendant figures in paint-splashed jeans – and Anne.

No Strings Attached

On that first morning she came down, skirt swinging in the wind, dark hair escaping from the old yachting cap, a satchel of charcoal sticks, Ingres paper and other materials over her shoulder.

She stepped lightly across the waste of silt, exchanging greetings with gnarled fishermen, their faces split in toothy grins. Moving swiftly among the stools dotted about the anchorage she plied a brisk trade with the lazy holiday painters.

It was only three days later that he got into conversation with her. She lived at Malvern, doing very little but look after her mother, a permanent invalid, and the house.

She sat opposite him in the little seafront café and sketched a swift picture of her life there, dull and monotonous, chained to the rambling old mansion. Apparently her whole existence had been spent on a stage-set of dusty twilit rooms against the lovely cyclorama of the Malvern Hills, a bubble of shadow in an ocean of sunlight.

When her father had suddenly, astonishingly, offered to look after his wife unaided for a while she had taken an excursion coach to St Ives, acquired a small stock of brushes and acrylic colours and started to peddle them round the dunes and alleyways where itinerant artists sat.

He went walking with her, exploring the coves and inlets concealed by the towans near Hayle. They bathed in the gentle waves, bronzed in the sun and bathed again.

They fell in love, kissed and argued and made up again till the little coloured weather-card turned from pink to blue, the days shortened and were lost in a seaweed-scented haze, and the letter arrived. It was her mother – a relapse. It was the end.)

"... *contents of pockets: one ballpoint pen, one cigarette case, empty, one leather wallet containing thirty-five pounds in notes, return half of a ticket to Malvern Wells* . . ."

Trial by Conscience

(Malvern Wells. The tiny station, clinging to the side of the hill as if bound to it by the gleaming curves of rail, dreaming of the days when dark green locomotives puffed importantly above the plain. The buildings echoed his footsteps as he paced up and down, a cigarette burning unchecked between his fingers. It was like her to arrange a rendezvous at a railway station where no trains came.

She met him at noon, a plaid scarf twisted loosely about her throat, handling two labradors with firm affection. They walked up over the grassy slopes, past the twinkling reservoir near the road to Ledbury, up to the beaconed skyline.

The dogs seemed to point her attitude of release, bounding joyfully through the bracken, stopping to sniff at the base of a gorse bush, trotting back tails a-quiver and dashing off again at their approach.

Down the path came a slim angular man, astute of face and dapper of clothing, reserve and a certain slyness in his bearing. The introductions were made, hastily, anxiously. "Father, this is Dick. I've told you about him. I met him in Cornwall . . ."

On to the house where he had never expected to set foot, to see her mother, a bedridden martyr, to feel the atmosphere of reproach and sarcasm. To catch, in a revelatory moment, the change in her father's expression, as he turned away from the invalid bed, from ineffable courtesy to – what? Agonized sadness? Dark, compassionate resolution?

Here Anne became different. She was subdued and almost fearful, a nonentity, yet tied to her mother by an unreasoning devotion and to her father by filial duty. Him he befriended by design. Out of interest burgeoning into fascination he talked to him, played chess with him and helped him with the hundred-and-one sick-room tasks which he shared with Anne in addition to his solicitor's work.

But he learned nothing of the man's feelings, towards his wife or his daughter. It was as if a robot ran the house and responded to the routine stimuli of daily living. Richard's one thought was to get Anne away – away from some impending disaster, both unknown and unimaginable.)

"... *your lawyer. You may refuse to see him if you wish, but it is recommended* ..."

(To get her away, that was the thing; to get back to the carefree happiness they had shared by the sea.

Lawyer? Why should he want a lawyer? He had done nothing – she had taken the car and driven away, that was all. The harsh unshaded light in the cell hurt his eyes; the stone walls were hostile – no, almost friendly. They mellowed the light and graded it through soft shades of amber and rose.

The lamplight softened the texture of the wall but it was rough to his hand as he kissed her and asked her to marry him, leaning against it in the fine Worcestershire rain. She clung to him with a force he had never suspected, then raised her head and studied him, her wide-set brown eyes warm and serious. Then she smiled and nodded, and misty chimes from the abbey were about them as he held her.

A fortnight later he was alone in London.)

"... *in the case of Regina v. Richard Henry Derwent on the eleventh day of December, nineteen hundred and* ..."

(A trial. He could see Anne's father below him, shuffling papers with a look of untouchable content. Beside him a well-fed cheek and an off-white wig nodded solemnly. He looked round the court, interested. A high-ceilinged room, sentinel windows and an impersonal human flavour – like the upper room in that Malvern house.

Anne's mother lay inert in the narrow bed, her wasted form hardly lifting the stiff brocade of the counterpane. She was dying;

didn't they see that? His mind jinked, events tumbled through his brain.

Anne and he had announced their engagement. When the old woman seemingly suffered a stroke at the news Anne would not leave. Both he and her father prevailed upon her. Nothing more could be done. Eventually she agreed and they got away not long after the doctor's sleek Daimler had purred round the corner.

At last Anne seemed free. She gave herself to him desperately, as though she were trying to find in him what had left her when she was able to cut loose the burden of her mother's care.

They were married in London. His best man said little and her father was not present. The next evening they were to leave for the Riviera and their honeymoon.

The telephone call came in the evening. It was her father, wishing them 'bon voyage' so Anne said, but she was disturbed and told him nothing more of the conversation except that her father had promised to ease her mother's sufferings. It was as if he were making sure that they were really going, he thought.

The following morning she was in a strange mood, strained and nervous, turning to him again and again with tense despair. He wondered if every bride was as nervous at the beginning of a new existence. She went out early to buy some flowers. She did not come back.)

"... *at the bar. Stand up. You are charged with* . . ."

(It was only later, making enquiries, that he learned that his car had gone from the hotel garage. He knew intuitively where she was going and was numbed by the realisation.

The notification of the fatal crash at Pershore did not move him. He remained numb. She had been within sight of her Malvern Hills. As the apple orchards slid past the train windows he did not even know why he was going back.)

"... *you plead 'Guilty' or 'Not Guilty'?*"

(Now he must tell them. About her father's furtive trip to the chemist; about his promise to ease suffering. About Anne's devotion. About the planted prescription. About his own inability to live without her.

He must tell the avuncular constable, her portly cousin who had appeared like a ghostly friar at the funeral, even her sad-eyed labradors – tell them that he had not tampered with the car, that he knew nothing of her vast inheritance through her mother's will, that he loved her. That he would love and cherish her till the end of time . . .)

"*Guilty, my lord.*"

R.O. and F.C.

My Uncle Hubert is a Queen's Counsel, and a pretty grand one at that. He is jolly and rotund, more of a Rumpole than a Marshall Hall, but his thunderings to the bench have to be heard to be believed, so they say.

On Sunday afternoons he often used to come to tea but the conversation with my mother and my aunt was stupefyingly bland and aimless. It reduced me to boredom. I longed to hear of some of his triumphs, and maybe disasters, in court; I had an idea that this was the stuff of life, the nitty-gritty, as distinct from the decorous tea table and the predictable scones with bramble jelly. I felt sure that there were stories to be told.

Finally one weekend there came the chance I had been hoping for. Aunt Daisy felt unwell and she and my mother disappeared into the house to pore over the little bottles in the bathroom cabinet.

Without hesitation I begged Uncle Hubert to tell me about some case or other that stood out in his memory – maybe even helped to shape his career. I waited breathlessly while he sank his chin onto his chest and pondered.

"I don't know about shaping my career," said Uncle Hubert, "but there was a case, very trivial in itself, that happened many years ago. It didn't produce great drama or turn on a fine point of law. Nevertheless I've always remembered it because it reminds me, when I need reminding, that legal tussles are not always won by the wiliest advocates. Sometimes victory can be achieved by conducting things badly. And of course it's always satisfying when the amateur can triumph over the professional. Would you care to hear about it?"

I nodded eagerly.

It all happened way back in the early sixties (he said) in Karachi, which at that time was the capital of the newly-formed Pakistan. There had been a great inrush of Muslims from India and the city was choked. Apart from the housing shortage the most immediate effect was on the traffic. It was a nightmare.

You may have leapt for your life on the Champs-Elysées or dodged a Cairo taxi but you have never tackled the Bunder Road in Karachi at sunset. This Bunder Road was wide and straight, a credit to those, living in the suburbs to which it led, who paid for it. But downtown, where the market stalls encroached on the dusty gutters and reduced the pavements to tunnels, the most intrepid driver was given food for thought.

The basic ingredient in the ever-boiling stew was the cycle rickshaw. That simple vehicle, no more than an elongated tricycle with a gaily painted box holding a double seat at the rear, was at once the cause and the victim of most of the tyre-screaming confusion.

There were hundreds of these fragile gadabouts, unhampered by more than the slightest gradient. With their ability to travel at 20 mph and execute right-angled turns at not much less they were a ubiquitous menace.

The drivers, pedalling away, were not ignorant of hand signals. However these were not used for changes of speed or direction. In fact there was only one signal. It consisted in holding an arm out pointing straight forward and was generally used for the

R.O. AND F.C.

lightning crossing of a main street, from invisibility to invisibility in seconds.

The other ingredients were a mixed lot. Ancient diesel trams rode into battle upon sulphurous clouds of their own exhausts, scattering bicycles and handcarts before them. A herd of water buffalo, a couple of oxcarts and a sacred cow or two, relic of Hindu rule, thickened the pot. And over all the rest, bobbing in an aloof and senseless pattern, the heads of the camels pulling grain floats to the docks seemed to comment on the recipe.

Actually it was not in Bunder Road itself but by the polo ground that my turn came. In those days the two of us, Gerald and I, ran a sturdy motorcycle; it was a 350 cc Velocette which suited the conditions and the temperature as well as anything else.

Two miles it was, from home to office and office to home, four times a day until we could ride it blindfold. But one evening the teratoid traffic pounced.

Between McLeod and Hoshang roads en route for Bath Island the roundabout where Queens Road entered was the only obstacle. I approached it at a decorous 20 mph, cleared the rear of a baker's van, found an elderly cycle rickshaw flashing across my path with arm outstretched, braked, sounded the horn and hit it squarely amidships, all in a matter of moments.

Gerald, who had tumbled more or less unscathed from the pillion, showed himself master of the situation. While I sat on the edge of the traffic island with my head in my hands he coped with the *dramatis personae*.

He attended to the rickshaw cyclist, who was lying in a conspicuously unconscious pose, produced taxis for his passengers (and money to compensate for dhobiing the cushions) and told a policeman in faultless Urdu that we would reserve our defence. The casualty was whisked away to the 7th day Adventist hospital;

I retrieved and inspected the motorbike and awaited the police inspector.

He arrived on foot, accompanied by two thin clerks with notebooks and measuring tapes. Having diagrammed the accident with care he requested me to take him back to his station on my pillion.

Feeling this to be a remarkable display of trust on his part I took the opportunity to demonstrate my roadcraft. My handling was immaculate, my hand signals clearly timed and executed and the gears changed like cream. Unfortunately this officer took no further part in the case.

At the police station a second officer was routed out to test the motorcycle. He wobbled uncertainly round the police compound on it and re-entered to made his report. From behind his desk he regarded me with bloodshot eyes.

"Front brake no good, you know," he began ominously. I gulped. "But we needn't mention that – nothing to do with it, really." I breathed again. "Rear one's the thing, isn't it?

"Hell of a hangover I've got, man. Carew's gin. Brother-in-law just in from Quetta. Hell of a party, man." I commiserated and mentioned the hair of the dog. We agreed to have a sundowner at the Sind Club.

Clutching my 'sound mechanical condition' report I arrived at the station captain's desk. "Just a few particulars," he said. "Father's name, mother's religion, drunk or sober . . ." I wondered whether he meant my parents or me. Another Mr Jingle, evidently.

While he filled in an enormous grey form I attempted to discover what action he intended to take. After a quarter of an hour or so it transpired that he was willing to prosecute. "Occupation?" he enquired, moving on to the next line.

"Law clerk," I replied, "but you don't mean that you're going to make a court case out of this little impingement, I mean infringement?"

"No choice. P.P.C. What was your occupation?"

"Jurisprudential apprentice," I said flatly. As I left the station he was still trying to get it into the small box provided on the grey form.

P.P.C. was the Pakistan Penal Code, originally modelled on the British code of justice. It might have been one of the institutions of Elphinstone himself. Gerald and I were there to study and advise on it; I knew that if I had fallen into its clutches there was no short cut to freedom.

The next day I was told officially to arraign myself before the magistrate's bench the following week and was released upon a thousand rupees bail, put up by a friend in the High Commission. In the event he left the country well before the trial and could never have been held to account for any defection. For the time being, however, I remained worried.

An interview with a crafty-looking agent of the insurance company, cheering reports from the hospital (the rickshaw driver had been detained only a couple of hours) and a visit to a practising lawyer friend passed the days away. Over dinner at the Boat Club he advised me to take no legal advice until the position became clear.

"Isn't that legal advice in itself?" I suggested. He bent a look at me over a forkful of rice. "Anyway, I'm supposed to be studying law," I went on. "Why don't I have a go at representing myself? Might be a lot of laughs!"

He became earnest. I had not been officially charged as far as he knew and all sorts of things could be thought up or added on in the meantime. All sorts of things, he emphasised, a sardonic eyebrow lending foreboding to the remark. Had I known what was to come I would have retained him on the spot.

On the day appointed I secured leave of absence from my law firm and arrived, punctually and innocently, at the barrack-like court house just off Bunder Road. Here was a side of the city that I had never seen before.

Great stone verandas, lined with barred grilles like Joliet, rose up one side of the building and on these the teeming life of the courts unfolded its diurnal plots.

Litigants and witnesses in shirts, *lungis* and *burquas* (tent-like cloaks with eye holes) squatted and sprawled over the spacious corridors or hung over the balustrade. Children and young goats were everywhere, prisoners chained by the waists and ankles stood along the walls and guarding them were smart recruits with rifles.

Preying upon the throng came the lawyers, dusty black coats and once-white bands a concession to their office. Came too the sellers of tea and of sweetmeats, tapping their trays underneath with brass-ringed fingers. Letter-writers sat at folding desks with rows of coloured fountain pens.

And then there were the wax-men. These were equipped with steel rods like knitting needles and quantities of cotton wool; their patrons squatted before them while they excavated in first one ear and then the other. The noise, the heat and the dust were without end.

After much delay the public prosecutor invited me into his cubby-hole of an office. He was a large greasy man with a small greasy Jinnah cap on the back of his head and a permanently confidential manner.

He spoke largely of his admiration for the British and our mutual friendship, casually mentioning that I was to be charged with causing injury on the highway and with driving recklessly and without due care and attention. He suggested quite boldly that I plead guilty to the first charge. He told me winningly that

R.O. AND F.C.

I should be fined not more than fifty rupees and he would not press the second charge.

It was my first experience of plea bargaining. Had I known more of the courts and their ways I might have considered this bribe but in my quasi-legal position I feared to agree to anything that smacked of bending the law. For all I knew he might be trying me out. The previous day the injured man's friends and family had tried to extort money from me but I had referred them smartly to the crafty insurance agent.

I decided to temporise. "But how can I plead guilty when I am not guilty?" I said as ingenuously as I could. At this effrontery the prosecutor blew through pursed lips, gathered his papers together in an evil manner and paced out of the room into court. A few minutes later the case came on.

I entered hesitantly. A spacious room with ceiling fans contained a raised dais bearing the magistrate and his clerk; the dock, two tables and numberless aged chairs were strewn in front.

The court was full of people and my impression was that all of them were talking at once. I learned later that it was customary to conduct three or four cases simultaneously to save time; disengaged lawyers and their clients either conferred murmurously or joined with interest in whatever portions of other cases were being heard at the time. Bow Street it wasn't.

As I stood uncertainly for a moment near the entrance a nearby advocate turned to me. "You are witness?" he observed. I nodded. "You over there," he pointed. I moved to the far side and sat down gingerly.

The clerk caught sight of me. "You are accused, no?" he enquired. I acquiesced. "You should be behind that table," he said. I moved again.

Finally the magistrate looked up. "Case 32. Where is defending counsel?" he asked. I stood up and smiled politely. "Come forward by the bench, please," he said. Advocate and clerk looked baffled.

To this day I believe that I owe life and liberty to the fact that most of those in court never quite recognised that I was witness, defendant and solicitor rolled into one. The magistrate was the only one alive to the position and even he had difficulty with knowing in what capacity he was addressing me at any one time.

Eventually he came to relish the situation and began to invent new and confounding variations upon it while the crooked prosecutor was switched and balked by turns, in mounting fury. But if the cats were temporarily at odds the mouse had still to find its escape.

On the first day the prosecution got under way with the evidence of the police. I learned for the first time that the policeman to whom Gerald had spoken had actually been leaning against a telegraph pole at the roundabout and had seen the whole thing. If he overestimated my speed I was done.

I was able to exploit some confusion in his account between the speed at which I was moving when he first saw me and the speed with which we had crunched into the rickshaw. Even so I was cast as the wicked aggressor in his story.

Luckily, however, it turned out that he should have been on point duty at the time instead of idling. The greasy prosecutor glared at him even more balefully than he did at me; out of the corner of my eye I could see the magistrate crossing the policeman's evidence out of his notes.

I became aware that all the state witnesses had prepared statements of their evidence and it was next to impossible to get them to change a word. They always finished with a flourish of "R.O. & F.C.!" which puzzled me. It wasn't until the last day of the trial that I discovered that it stood for Read Over and Found Correct.

R.O. AND F.C.

The police submitted the diagram of the accident and the magistrate warned me that he would probably base his judgment largely on it. Did I wish to challenge it? I saw no point in doing so. Thus ended the first day. The case was postponed for five weeks and I returned to circulation.

Soon afterwards I learned from the crafty insurance agent that he had had the rickshaw repaired and paid the driver's small hospital bill, with which he had declared himself satisfied.

In my innocence I was perturbed. "You had no right to do that!" I protested. "That's tantamount to admitting my liability for the accident! When the court hears of this they will take it that in your opinion it was my fault. In any case, whatever the driver signed, there's nothing to prevent his lawyer from asking for damages when he sums up."

The agent apologised, still craftily, and explained that as they operated on a 'knock-for-knock' basis with other insurance companies and as this man was uninsured they made the 'third party' payment automatically. Anyway, he couldn't earn his living without his rickshaw, he added.

So the driver was back on the road, I noted. His injuries couldn't have been in any way serious.

The second day of the trial came round. More police gave evidence, R.O. & F.C. The hungover officer who had tested the motorbike put in his report and a young Bengali constable described how he had arrived on the scene a few minutes after the crash. He had found his father lying in the road soaked in blood, he said brokenly.

My own blood ran cold. That the driver's son should be a policeman and that he should be at the scene so rapidly was a perverse quirk of fate. No wonder the police captain had been forced to charge me.

This zealous lad giving evidence had not seen his father's

reckless assault on the fast line of traffic, only the piteous sight of him lying injured in the road. I thought of querying why he was in the witness box at all, since he was not present at the material time, but considered it prudent, on reflection, to ask him no questions.

Another adjournment followed, of four weeks. By this time our return to London was pending and the head of the firm was demanding to know why the affair was dragging on.

At the next hearing I waited all day outside the seedy court. Six and a half humid hours passed. Then I found that the usher had called my first name in the corridor and that I had not responded. When I heard his pronunciation of my name I suggested that the court should not be surprised.

Nevertheless the doctor had been ready to give evidence and had now gone away again. Was I to be held in contempt of court? The magistrate pronounced another adjournment and observed in meaningful tones that he would reserve his decision. Obviously, one more incident and I was finished.

On the trial's third day the doctor reappeared, gave his evidence in a high Cumbrian monotone and vanished, managing to convey the impression of rushing from one life-and-death case to the next.

I got in one question before he departed. No, he didn't think the injuries were at all severe. I had hoped he would say that, being no doubt accustomed to much more serious cases at the hospital.

However this impression was soon dispelled by the appearance of the driver himself in the witness box. I could scarcely believe it was the same man.

The vigorous sexagenarian who had pedalled so fearlessly across the road junction had now become a pathetic and emaciated patient. Huge white bandages coiled round his forehead, his elbows and his shins, while his head nod-nodded in constant rhythm as he strove pitifully to follow the proceedings.

The magistrate studied this latest victim of the Imperialist regime while a certain hubbub rose from the court. It seemed that the old man spoke only Tamil, a language widely used but far from universally understood in this area.

The greasy prosecutor instantly demanded that I hire and pay for an interpreter. The magistrate cast suffering eyes at the ceiling fans and charitably offered to translate into Urdu and English. Was this a Greek gift, I wondered?

The old man's evidence was much as expected. He, an honest and law-abiding citizen, had been riding his valuable rickshaw slowly and carefully along the edge of the road when suddenly, mala! I was upon him like a four-man wind.

This drew a chuckle from the court, being a reference to the bunder boats – tall dhows with a plank projecting from the windward gunwale. According to the strength of the breeze the boat would be balanced by a man or boy squatting at the tip of the plank, eight feet out over the water; the fresher the breeze, the more plank squatters there were. A four-man blow was the strongest in which they would venture from harbour.

While he was gaining the sympathy of the crowd I came across a vital point on the back of my linen driving licence which I had been idly scanning. I rose and addressed him through the magistrate.

"Did he hear me sound my horn?"

"No."

"Did he see me approaching?"

"No." He began to look more eager – I was only strengthening his case. I played my new-found trump.

"Did he know the traffic rule that all traffic must give way to vehicles approaching from the right?"

The magistrate glanced up sharply. "Were you coming from his right?" he said quickly. With a gesture I referred him to the police diagram. The prosecutor looked thunderously at the witness who cringed visibly. I felt that I had at last opened the scoring.

The court rose for lunch and the magistrate beckoned me behind the screen at the back of the bench. While he tucked a napkin under his collar and settled down to a platter of curry we chatted of this and that. Then he came to the point.

I was an amateur actor of the Karachi Theatre, was I not? He indicated a picture on the back page of *Dawn* showing myself with Valerie D—- in a scene from Strindberg's *Playing With Fire*. Val was showing a lot of leg.

Could I get him tickets for this play? There was no 'legit' theatre in Karachi at that time and no doubt he imagined on the strength of the photograph that the show was sort of Bacchanalian orgy.

I thought rapidly. We had given only a few performances for members in the producer's house but there had been a rumour that when Mr Mohammad Ali returned from Calcutta there might be a request performance at his official residence.

"I'm not sure. Do you know the Prime Minister?" I asked casually. Taken aback, he shot a glance at his aide.

"Well, no, actually. But I knew the last one," he said hopefully. I promised to see what I could do. I implied that I would speak to Mohammad Ali personally if necessary.

The prosecution was now finished. Five more weeks passed and we reassembled to hear my defence. My only witness was Gerald. Standing easily in the box in his spotless whites he gave a sober and reasonable account of the accident. I rose to round off his evidence neatly.

"And you would not say, would you, that there was anything

more than I could conceivably have done to avoid this wild rickshaw?" I smiled, confidently. Gerald paused to make sure of giving a completely true and honest answer.

"Well, you could have swerved round him, I suppose," he offered cheerfully.

There was an appalling silence. Diabolical triumph creased the prosecutor's face and the magistrate gazed delicately into a far corner.

Somehow I got honest, uncomprehending Gerald off the stand and entered my own plea. Desperately I drew attention to the tyre marks, proving that I had braked violently, the scratches on the road showing how little the rickshaw had slid and the insignificant damage (one headlamp glass) testifying to the gentleness of the impact. "R.O. & F.C.!" I declared with the air of a magic spell. It went off like a damp squib.

The greasy prosecutor, by this time so confident that he scarcely bothered to contest my statements, wound up in rolling English periods interspersed with humorous Urdu asides to his sycophants, convulsing them. The case was over and the magistrate closed his notebook.

Diffidently I enquired the verdict. It was an optimistic question. A final huge adjournment of seven weeks was announced. I nearly offered to pay the fine there and then to save time.

But in the end it was all right. When the 'findings' day came the magistrate discharged me without ceremony. I've never forgotten his final words.

"Possibly," he said drily, "if you had conducted your case a little better you would have been found guilty!"

Friendly Relations

WILLIAM PERKINS sat on the old wooden garden seat and thought deeply about his problem. All about him the sights and sounds of the countryside spoke of a comfortable mellow autumn. The few remaining roses nodded in the late afternoon warmth of the patio flagstones while the summer jasmine reached out to him from the wall with inquisitive tendrils.

On the lawn around the patio the ordered bands of dark and pale green showed that Jonathan had been busy with mower and hose. Starlings argued and chased each other round the silver willow while in the background the first few leaves of birch and sycamore twirled lazily downwards.

Beyond the garden William could hear shouts and laughter from the apple pickers in the orchard, punctuated by the rusty bray of the donkey who lived there. The air was still.

It was a pretty scene in the golden sunshine – a very pretty scene, William thought. It was really an ideal time to have moved from town to country and he had had a few weeks to get used to his new surroundings. And yet he was not content.

It wasn't so much the upheaval of the move. Alicia had told him about it while patting him consolingly on the head.

"Listen, William, Gordon and I have to go abroad for a few months so you're going to live with Uncle Jonathan in Leicestershire for a while. You'll like that. Good country food and lots of new friends. And more space to play in than we have here. You'll be a good boy till we get back, won't you?"

William knew that the overseas trip was something to do with the pictures of gaunt Balkan children in Alicia's newspaper. She talked about bringing people together through an agency called Friendly Relations; it was obvious that he, William, was not going to be involved. He wondered what was going to happen to him until Alicia explained it all; a few days later Jonathan arrived to take him to his new home.

He liked Jonathan well enough. Jonathan was elderly and absent-minded and rather set in his ways but he made William comfortable and didn't fuss over him. He left him free to explore the neighbourhood and didn't exclaim or cast his eyes to the ceiling if William came in late from his evening stroll. The house was beautifully appointed and spotlessly clean. All in all, it was quite a cosy bachelor establishment.

Except for the food, that was. Jonathan evidently regarded eating as a repetitive process, like morning shaving, that was best reduced to a routine and disposed of as quickly as possible. The idea of a varied and appetizing diet, let alone an occasional treat, found no place in his philosophy.

Surrounded as he was by the meats, fruits and vegetables of the country he subsisted mainly on bread and jam, weak tea and shapeless morsels that came from the local mini-market in cardboard packets with happy chefs pictured on them.

William rapidly became disenchanted with weak tea and anonymous cereals. He longed for some stewed steak or a leg of chicken slathered in gravy, with maybe a few fancy biscuits to follow.

He ruefully remembered Alicia's steamed fish dishes; the smell alone made his mouth water. Jonathan had no time for preparing fish, not even a simple kipper fillet with a dab of parsley butter. William sighed heavily.

A few days ago, however, he had discovered a possible alternative. Returning from one of his walks he was passing the driveway of a rather tumbledown bungalow further down the road when a motherly figure called to him.

"Hallo, you're William, aren't you? Come to stay with Jonathan at the corner? How do you like village life, then? A bit quieter than the city, isn't it? Tell you what, I've got something you'll like; come round to the back door."

William cautiously followed her round the bungalow and was astonished and delighted to find two salmon sandwiches awaiting him on an earthenware plate. Not only that, he had company. Sitting near the plate was a vision of feminine enchantment with long silky hair and clear green eyes. He glanced at her but she affected not to notice him.

"There you are, this is Lucy," said the motherly figure. "Say hallo nicely. Lucy didn't want all her elevenses this morning, did you Lucy? Such a waste to throw it away. Tuck in, William, have as much as you like."

William fell to with a will. After he had polished off the salmon Lucy unbent and they got to know each other. Together they wandered off to explore the nooks and corners of the neglected property.

They played hide-and-seek in the shrubbery and flopped, exhausted, onto a sofa in the summerhouse. Later they came in from the garden and invented a game that involved chasing a bouncy rubber ball up and down the hall and skidding hilariously on the lino. William enjoyed every minute.

Now, however, he had his problem to contend with. Over the past few days the picture had come into focus. The banquets at the shabby bungalow down the road, to say nothing of Lucy's alluring company, drew him back again and again.

He took to spending guilty hours there, only to wonder at

himself when he returned to the neatness and quiet of Jonathan's house and garden. He felt uneasy about the situation. Also, Jonathan began to notice his long absences.

"You've been down to Margaret's again, haven't you?" he remarked to William as he put a bowl of unmentionable bran, mashed banana and milk in front of him.

"I suppose Lucy's the attraction, eh? Yes, she's quite bewitching in her way. Margaret and I used to get on well before Lucy arrived. At one time I thought there was a chance that we might – well, anyway, all her time is taken up with Lucy these days. That's how it goes."

William didn't see why that should be how it went. Life, he realised, was very much a matter of food and shelter, even in a sophisticated community. Jonathan's shelter was beyond reproach but Margaret's cooking could not be ignored.

He didn't want to spend the next few months trotting up and down the village road between them. There was a solution, of course. Somehow these two people must be brought together. But how?

He shifted and stretched on the garden seat as an idea began to form in his mind. He examined it judiciously and found no snags. The idea was simple to implement, required no elaborate planning and would surely be effective. It needed only Lucy's consent and co-operation. He strolled off down the road in the light of the setting sun to exercise his powers of persuasion.

The evening lengthened into a hushed dusk as William and Lucy communed in the summerhouse. Margaret came out to put some scraps in the dustbin and disappeared. Down the road Jonathan went absent-mindedly to bed. One by one the lights in the village went out.

The following morning a white police car pulled into the bungalow driveway. A fresh-faced young constable got out and rang the doorbell. Behind him Jonathan emerged from the car carrying a bundle.

"Good morning, madam," the constable said to the motherly figure in the doorway. "We have something of yours, I believe. This gentleman's got it."

Margaret clasped her hands and tears came to her eyes. "Oh, Lucy! It *is* Lucy, isn't it? She didn't come home last night. I was so worried. Thank goodness you found her! Where was she?"

Jonathan came forward and gently placed the bundle in Margaret's arms. "This officer saw the two of them crouched by the side of the road on the other side of the village, miles from anywhere," he said. "Lucy was with William. Luckily William had his collar on with his name and address so he brought them both straight back."

"Yes, I don't know what they were doing," said the young policeman. "Eloping, perhaps? Cats do tend to wander off from time to time, don't they? If I were you I'd keep them in for a few days. Good morning, madam; morning, sir."

William, peering out of the car window, noticed the looks exchanged by Jonathan and Margaret and saw Jonathan place a protective arm round her. She seemed to nestle against him.

Mission accomplished, he thought. Bed and breakfast forever with the delectable Lucy. He yawned and curled up, satisfied. Alicia would be pleased with his exercise in friendly relations.

Weather Watch

CHRISTA was glad to find the cheap bed-sitter in Rotherhithe. It was advertised optimistically as a studio – probably on account of the large north-facing window, she thought. It turned out to be merely a square unfurnished room on the top floor of a remarkably ugly brick building.

There was a battered cooker covered in dust and a shower cubicle in one corner but that was all. However she was glad to find that by craning out of the north window she could see Tower Bridge to the left and a skyscraper on the Isle of Dogs the other way. At least it was a room with a view.

She discovered that the ugly building was a converted warehouse divided into small units. They were doubtless intended for light industrial use but in many cases the owner both worked and made a home there.

On one side of her lived a youngish man with freckles and an engaging smile. He introduced himself as Eddie Roach, maker of costume jewellery for the not-too discerning. "Roach the brooch!" he laughed.

On the other side a nameplate with the one word 'Liebermann' on an unvarnished door gave little away. However through the thin dividing wall she could hear rasping and tapping from time to time, suggesting some activity in wood and metal.

Occasionally scraps of conversation were audible but Christa did not turn down her TV to listen. She didn't want to be known as a nosy neighbour.

She enjoyed furnishing her room. Her bed came up in a spacious goods lift and Eddie manhandled the small wardrobe and chest of drawers into position. A folding table, two chairs and some scattered rugs completed the essentials.

Not long afterwards she met her other neighbour, emerging from the lift. He was a portly middle-aged figure in a rumpled tweed coat. His hair was ruffled and his pink jowls shook slightly as he moved. He halted abruptly and studied her not unkindly through his half-moon pince-nez.

"Liebermann!" he said, confirming the nameplate. "You are the new tenant, *ja*? Is good. Today ve haf sun but tomorrow vill come rain. Excuse me, please." He vanished into his room, leaving Christa amused and speechless.

Over the next week or two she and Eddie got to know each other. He bought her a few drinks in the Surrey Docks Tavern and she baked him a couple of cakes in the now dustless cooker. He was duly grateful, explaining that he often forgot to eat when creating some adornment or other.

"I still don't know what *you* do," he remarked one evening over a pint.

"Give you three guesses!" she said.

"Let's see," Eddie mused. "You're quietly dressed and you don't wear a ring or any other jewellery. I could help you there, by the way. You don't carry a briefcase and you sometimes complain of aching feet. You come home late about twice a week and you never speak of an office or a restaurant."

"Very observant," said Christa. "You must have been watching me. Are you writing a report?"

"No, no," Eddie replied. "Although I'd be quite happy to. Watch you, I mean." He pursed his lips. "Now, why did you mention a report? I know – you're a rookie journalist. Or you're a food inspector, or a policewoman."

"Close, but no cigar!" said Christa. "Actually I'm a trainee store detective. At Hampson's, in the West End. I mingle with the shoppers and try to spot those light fingers."

Eddie's eyebrows lifted. "Really? Sounds intriguing. By the way, Hampson's take some of my necklaces. You won't let them go walkabout, will you?"

Christa shook her head. "Leave it to me, Watson; you know my methods. So – we know what you and I do for a living, but what about my other neighbour? I don't want to be inquisitive but it would be nice to have some idea of how he supports himself."

"Otto Liebermann? He's a mystery," said Eddie. "He's from Austria, I believe, but nobody knows what he does. On the few occasions when we've met he always says something about the weather. 'Strong vinds today from the vest. A mild night ve shall haf!'"

Christa chuckled. "You're naughty!" she said. "Tell you what, though. With our combined talent for observation we ought to be able to discover Herr Liebermann's secret. Shall we have a go? Or would that be out of order?"

"No, that's all right," said Eddie. "Why not? Good clean fun. But we're not allowed to ask him – or anyone else. Fair's fair."

Christa didn't learn much over the following weeks. Once she overheard a voice from next door. Mr Liebermann was muttering loudly that someone called Gerald was proving a nuisance. Gerald, it seemed, was preventing him from making progress with someone else called Lucy.

"So beautiful she is in her summer dress vith the pretty parasol I gave her. Such a picture! I fall more in love vith her every day." His tone grew darker. "But that Gerald, he is the problem. Vat can I do about him?" Christa didn't hear an answer to the question.

She and Eddie compared notes. Eddie had come across Mr Liebermann in a hardware store buying brass hinges and a roll of sheet lead. He had scuttled out of the shop before Eddie could get close to him.

"I've noticed a smell of glue," said Christa. "What on earth can he be doing? Hinges and lead? You don't think – you don't think he's making a coffin, do you?"

Eddie wagged his head. "Unlikely," he said. "I mean, there's no evidence of a pet that's died, or anything like that. And he wouldn't be an undertaker, surely, up on the top floor of a building of this kind."

Nevertheless Christa's unease soon deepened. The janitor asked her if she was troubled by rats. "That foreign bloke next to you has bought a lot of rat poison, you know," he told her. "I thought you might have a problem."

Then there were the books. A parcel of them was left at Mr Liebermann's door and Christa noticed from the label that they included *A History of Forensic Medicine* and *Arsenic Murders of the Nineteenth Century*. What could interest him in books like those?

She confided her suspicions to Eddie when he dropped in for a cup of tea. "Whatever his occupation is, he's up to no good, I'm sure of it," she said. "The clues are all there; motive, means – all that's missing is opportunity!"

Suddenly from the next room came the familiar voice, now raised in frustration. "Ach, Gerald, it is no good. You vill not be as I vant. I cannot stand it any longer. Your umbrella vill not save you. *Mein Gott*, I vill finish you here and now!" There was a scrambling sound and a clear thud.

Christa and Eddie sprang up and dashed into the corridor.

Weather Watch

They looked at each other in alarm. Eddie paused for a moment and then broke open the unvarnished door with one powerful kick. The door swung back to reveal Mr Liebermann, looking startled and apprehensive, in a cluttered workshop.

"What's going on? Where's Gerald? What have you done to him?" cried Eddie. They stopped and looked round.

Clocks and barometers hung on the walls and the workbench was festooned with springs and cog wheels. At one end of it stood a small Tyrolean chalet with two doors, one marked *Lucy* and the other *Gerald*. Lucy, the fine weather girl, was half hidden but Gerald, a tiny rain-coated figure, was in Mr Liebermann's hand, about to be smashed.

Mr Liebermann glanced down at Gerald as if in answer to Eddie's questions. Then he looked up and surveyed the two of them, the expression of apprehension gradually melting into one of polite enquiry. He put his head on one side and waited.

Eddie and Christa both blushed. "I say, I'm terribly sorry for bursting in," Eddie said. "And for the damage to the door. I'll get it fixed, don't worry. I'm afraid I – we got you all wrong. You see, we watched closely but . . ."

Otto Liebermann looked quizzical. "Maybe in future you vatch only the veather, like me. Is good?"

Happy Like Us

On his small tiled balcony Arthur Pennicutt shifted uneasily in his favourite chair and stared out over the Mediterranean. The sun blazed down persistently on the white walls and red-orange roofs of the Spanish fishermen's cottages near the beach. The roadway in between shimmered with heat. It was going to be another scorching day.

By leaning forward he could almost see the far-off spot where the disaster had occurred last night. His car was out of sight at the back but in any case he didn't want to look at it. There might be tell-tale signs of what had happened.

Arthur sucked in one corner of his mouth despondently and wondered how he had come to be in his present plight. It was nearly ten years ago, he recalled, that he and Jane had taken the plunge. They had sold their drab little council flat in Redbridge, drawn all their savings from the building society and flown out to the Costa del Sol like so many others.

At first things had been difficult. They had stayed in the cheapest one-star *hostals* up and down the coast while they had looked for the villa of their dreams. They were accosted by timeshare salesmen and bewildered by advertisements in the local paper describing remote tumbledown farmhouses as superb country residences.

But there were no villas that they could afford. The market was dominated by wealthy Swedes and Germans, all of them after a holiday home with a swimming pool and ready to pay well for it.

Finally they found an apartment block still under construction and hastily put down a deposit on a two-bedroom flat with an ocean view. It wasn't a dream villa but they would be able to sunbathe on the balcony and swim in the communal pool whenever they wanted.

While they waited for the Spanish workmen to finish their plastering and tiling Arthur found a job in a local language school, as he had planned, and Jane spent happy hours choosing curtain fabrics and chair covers, improving her colloquial 'Andaluz' in the process.

The apartment was in one of the new *urbanizaciones* between Estepona and Gibraltar, near the southern tip of Andalucia. The estate was occupied more by foreigners than by Spaniards but they came to be accepted by the community, who were more than willing to sell them the cheap clothes and vegetables and Moroccan gewgaws that covered the stalls in the village market. In fact Arthur felt comfortably at home until the tragedy.

He remembered the day, three years back, when Jane had complained of stomach pains and had gone to lie down. Arthur was not too worried; they had both had trouble, earlier on, with impure water or half-cooked shellfish or whatever and had suffered the usual upsets. Things were better now. When he looked in later, however, he was alarmed to find that she was moaning in agony and barely conscious.

In a panic he had telephoned the *Servicio de Urgencia*. An ambulance arrived and Jane was taken away on a stretcher. He followed the ambulance to the hospital in Marbella and waited in a noisy ill-furnished visitors' room; telephones rang, children squabbled and white-coated orderlies crossed back and forth with other patients on trolleys.

Eventually a grave, bearded English-speaking doctor had steered him to a small consulting room and broken the news. The medical emergency team had done all they could – had worked heroically, in fact – but they had been unable to save her. The truth broke on him. Jane was dead.

The doctor said something about poisoning and a death certificate but Arthur was too numbed to pay attention. Later on, however, when he had to cope with the funeral arrangements he found the ceremony was to be delayed. Apparently the hospital authorities were not wholly satisfied as to the cause of death.

Arthur was interviewed by the Marbella municipal police, then by a curt sly-talking lawyer and then a magistrate in his black gown. A quiet man from the British consulate in Malaga was involved for a time and the confusion seemed to increase by the day.

Eventually, however, someone in the judiciary seemed to yield and the necessary certificate was issued. Jane was interred in the British cemetery near St George's church and Arthur was left to pick up the pieces of his life.

But he did not feel at home as he once had. Word must have reached the *policia local* in the village and he was left in little doubt that he was under observation. Police patrol cars often passed by at walking pace and curious eyes scanned his balcony as if he were a suspect drug-runner.

Fortunately as the pain faded he came to know Euphemia in the next block. Euphemia was a vivacious widow who relieved the traditional black of her dress with a rather startling shade of red lipstick.

He learned that she was a native of Andalucia whose husband had died somewhere in Libya while working on a desalination plant. She existed on a small pension out of which she fed her three large dogs.

Euphemia took Arthur under her wing. Together they went

for strolls along the beach and bartered jointly in the village shops. From time to time they drove out into the country, stopping at a *venta* for lunch and returning home with bunches of roadside flowers.

Little by little Arthur relaxed. Euphemia, he found, was by nature tender and responsive, observing his moods and anticipating his wants with wonderful sympathy. The patrol cars crawled by less frequently and the market traders were more jovial than ever. Life was tranquil again.

Then it happened. Driving back from the language school in the dusk of the previous evening Arthur made his usual turn off the *carretera* towards the sea. Halfway along the narrow access road he was enveloped in a swirl of sand and dust picked up by the westerly wind.

It was in the cloud of dust that the impact occurred. He did not see anything but a solid body bounced off the nearside wing; he heard a choked-off cry and the car seemed to bump over something soft.

Arthur gripped the wheel in shock and fear. For a second time in his life he panicked. Without thinking he drove rapidly on out of the swirling dust, ran his car into its small garage space, took the lift up to his flat and reached for the telephone. On the point of dialling he froze.

What was he to say? That he'd run somebody over? That another person might have been killed in suspicious circumstances, to do with himself? Even worse, that he'd fled from the scene of the incident?

Arthur put down the receiver and dropped his face into his hands. What a fool he'd been! How could he have behaved so callously? Whoever it was on the narrow road might be injured and calling for help. They might even be dead!

Maybe the national police, the *guardia civil*, were already on the spot. He dared not go back and look. If they were, and learned of his involvement, he might be imprisoned for years. Years!

He trailed out to the balcony, sat down gazing dully at the distant glare of the lights of the fishing fleet and tried desperately to decide what to do. An anonymous telephone call to the police would be useless; the English accent would betray him and a routine check of the estate would soon reveal his identity. It was too late to wake Euphemia and even if he got her to make the call for him she would be unable to answer questions in detail.

Racked by guilt and indecision he had finally dropped off to sleep. Now it was morning again and the horror of his situation swept over him afresh. What was he to do?

A harsh buzz at the door made him jump. Surely the police could not be here already? How would they have known where to come? Maybe they had a file on him and were simply checking on him automatically. Clearly there was no escape.

He approached the door apprehensively and opened it, to reveal Euphemia looking downcast, unlike her usual cheerful mien. She sighed solemnly and came in, taking no notice of his strained expression. Sad or not, Euphemia was full of news, as always; she chattered on while Arthur listened to his own terrifying thoughts.

". . . and, you know, it is terrible but it is – how you say? – blessing in disguise. Poor Pedro, my oldest dog, was very sick. The *veterinario* was going to give him injection. To finish. But last night he gone out and I no find him.

"This morning he is discovered on the road. Someone hit him with car. Terrible! But he not suffer. He happy now, like us. No?"

The Guiding Light

Marjorie first heard the story of the guiding light when she was helping Peter, her father, to clear out the attic. It all began when they came upon a faded photograph among the old gramophone records and twisted squash racquets.

The photograph showed a young man in blazer and flannels with hair parted and smoothed flat, grinning into harsh sunlight. Hanging onto his arm was a girl in a sleeveless dress, smiling shyly. Behind the couple a stretch of water could be seen, covered in flat boats with rounded tops.

"Look, Dad, that's you and Mum!" Marjorie exclaimed. "Weren't you both slim? And Mum's dress – were they really that length? That was in Hong Kong, wasn't it, in the old days?"

"Hey, not so old, if you don't mind," Peter said. "Only twenty-five years ago, to be exact. Yes, that was Hong Kong. That picture was taken near Aberdeen harbour – you can see the sampans where the fisherfolk lived. And where they still live, come to that."

"That's where you met Mum, wasn't it? That's really romantic!"

"Yes, that's where I met my guiding light," Peter nodded. "But it was anything but romantic. Desperate would be a better word. In fact it started off as a drama and rapidly turned into a life-and-death episode."

Marjorie's eyes widened. "It did? How exciting! I didn't know that; you've never told me. What happened? And why do you call Mum your guiding light?"

"We couldn't tell you – or anyone else for that matter," Peter replied. "However, the risk is past now so there's no reason why you can't know the whole story. We always meant to tell you one day; in fact I wrote it all down not long ago. Let me see – yes, here it is."

Stretching over a tea-chest full of magazines he unearthed a sheaf of papers in a wrinkled box. He untied the string, blew off the dust and handed the papers to her. She recognised his neat, angular writing.

"I've put it in the form of a story," Peter explained. "At the time we didn't know all the details, of course. When we did, it was easier to tell the story in its proper sequence. Read it; then you'll know why Gill was my Heaven-sent guiding light."

Marjorie picked her way down the attic stairs, found a small bag of sweets and took them and the papers onto the terrace. She settled into a wicker chair, unwrapped a toffee and scanned the first page.

The end of the trade fair in Canton came as a blessed relief (she read). For the past three days Gillian seemed to have done nothing but hand out brochures, answer endless questions from earnest Chinese businessmen and cope with innumerable demands from her own team. They wanted Sellotape dispensers and label moisteners and batteries for dictation machines, none of which was available in the late sixties in Canton – or Kwang Chow, as she had learned to call the city.

The trade fair hall was hot and humid and the babble of Cantonese all around her smote her ears. Accompanying the sales team into this unknown land of southern China had been an intriguing opportunity but a wearying one. And when they had finally packed up their stand there was a banquet of many dishes and many toasts. By the time it ended she wanted nothing more than to get back to her spartan hotel and lie down.

Entering her room, Gillian switched on the ceiling fan and flopped onto the bed. At least it was quiet here, she reflected. Very different from the roar of central Hong Kong. In fact there were no city sounds such as she was used to. A constant tinkle of bicycle bells came faintly on the breeze, with an occasional 'bong' from a clock in a square turret across the rooftops.

She breathed more deeply and closed her eyes. The soft panting sound of the fan blades was soothing. But there was something else. She listened intently. A creak from the corridor was followed by a discreet tapping at her door.

Gillian sat up. Who could want to see her at this hour? It wouldn't be one of the hotel night staff, surely? A colleague from the team, perhaps? Thankful that she wasn't in her nightdress, or less, she put her shoes on and went across to open the door.

A young man stood there, hand still raised to tap. He looked somewhat dishevelled in his deep-pocketed shirt and khaki shorts and his face had a haggard look.

"I say, I'm terribly sorry to bother you," he said, "but could I possibly have a word? It's very urgent, believe me." He looked up and down the corridor. "If I could come in for a moment I'd be very grateful."

Gillian considered his pleasant, open features and chestnut hair. She noted the twinkle in his eyes and the pleading gesture of his hands. This was no hopeful Lothario, still less a nervy scheming rapist. She swung the door back and waved him into the room.

"Thanks awfully," he said. "I'm sorry to be a nuisance but I've got no one else to turn to." Gillian closed the door and they sat down on either side of a low table. "I saw you leaving the trade fair on your own and followed you. Hope you don't mind. The fact is, I want to ask you a favour. It's just a small thing, really."

He held out a small, flat packet. "You're leaving tomorrow, aren't you? Would you take this back to Hong Kong with you and post it to England? It's a message to my parents. They live in the country and haven't got a telephone. It's to tell them what's happened to me."

Gillian looked at him. "Just a message, is it?" she said. "Are you sure? No drugs, no currency, no contraband?"

"No, no, nothing like that," he said earnestly. "Look, you can open it when I've gone and see for yourself. It's just an account of what happened to me yesterday. My name's Peter by the way."

"I'm Gillian. This account of yours – it sounds rather ominous," she remarked. "What did happen to you yesterday? And why do you have to smuggle the story out to your parents?"

The young man slumped slightly in his chair. "I don't mind telling you all about it," he said, "if you have the time to listen. It's all in there, anyway. The whole unbelievable story." He laughed without any mirth.

"Yesterday morning I was happy and carefree, would you believe? I've been here for a month or so on an exchange tourist visa, cycling around the country for much of the time.

"A couple of days ago I was further up the Pearl River at Shiu Hing, taking some pictures of the bauhinias and camellias, when I was accosted by two brutal-looking types in dark blue uniforms. They tried to grab my camera and pointed to a wire fence and some low buildings in the middle distance. The place was probably a military installation of some kind.

"I didn't stop to argue. I sprang on the bike and pedalled off, leaving them shouting in the road. One of them sprinted after me but he soon gave up.

"After that I made my way towards Kwang Chow, thinking that I'd got away, but of course in China you're so conspicuous as a 'round-eye' Westerner. You can't melt into the background.

"I was riding as quickly as possible through a small village on the outskirts of the city when an elderly man in a grimy *cheong sam* seemed to fling himself across my path. Or more probably was flung. Anyway I couldn't avoid crashing into him. He went down in a heap and I fell off the bike.

"In an instant a crowd of villagers surrounded me, waving their fists and shrieking. Three of the blue-uniformed gang pushed through and got hold of me, confiscated my camera and marched me off to an ugly brick building where an older, grey-uniformed man was sitting at a desk.

"He had a few words of English, at least. I gathered that I was to be hauled up in front of a people's court charged with dangerous riding and causing injury on the highway – that kind of thing. I could do nothing about it.

"They let me go eventually but they took my passport and visa, and the pass which allowed me to travel round Kwang Tung province. I suppose I'm out on bail, you might say. The day after tomorrow I've got to go back and face the music."

"Well, I'm sorry you've got into a spot of trouble," Gillian said. "but things are not that bad, surely? You may be fined or something, but you don't need to sent urgent SOS messages, do you?"

Peter looked down at the table top. "I haven't told you the crucial part," he said. "Two of the blue-uniformed guards I saw at their headquarters were the same two who tried to arrest me at Shiu Hing! I recognised them.

"They were grinning evilly. I bet they set up the accident in the village; it was too obviously staged. But that was just a delaying tactic while they develop my film. They're going to charge me with espionage, I know. Taking pictures of military subjects.

"I don't mind so much losing the camera – it's only got picturesque views on the film – but languishing in a Chinese prison for a year or two, that's another matter. They'd do it, too. Similar things have happened before."

Gillian thought for a moment. She too had heard stories of foreigners being imprisoned by the Communist regime for minor misdemeanours. It was not a fate to contemplate with equanimity, especially in a remote village jail. She leaned forward over the table top, her lassitude gone.

"Just a minute," she said. "You've got until the day after tomorrow, you say? Well, why hang around? We're only about seventy miles from Shen Zhen, at the frontier. Why don't you make a dash for Hong Kong and freedom?"

Peter looked at her appreciatively. "For one so innocent in appearance you're pretty quick to flout the law," he said. "But it can't be done.

"I have no papers now so I can't get across the border. In fact, I'd probably be arrested at the railway station. This military-style regime, you know. They weren't afraid to let me out of their sight; they know I can't go far."

"Listen," said Gillian, "ordinary Chinese citizens have even less chance of getting travel documents but that doesn't stop them reaching Hong Kong. Thousands and thousands have made it – political dissidents, refugees and many simply looking for a better life. If they can do it, so can you."

"I can, can I?" Pete asked. "And just how would I go about it? I can't speak more than a few words of Cantonese and I've no money to buy forged papers. I don't even know where the line of the frontier is."

The Guiding Light

"You don't have to," Gillian said. "I'll tell you exactly what to do. The vital question is, can you swim? I mean more than a few strokes?"

"I can swim all right, at least I did at school; but I haven't done much since. If I've got to swim down the Pearl River, I've had it. The current is very powerful – I've seen it. I couldn't stay afloat."

Gillian shook her head. "Nothing like that. What you do is this. Find your way by back roads to the Sham Chun – that's a small river that forms much of the border between China and the New Territories of Hong Kong. The border itself is only about fifteen miles long; the train goes as far as a bridge in the middle.

"To the left as you approach it is Sha Tau Kok Hoi – Starling Inlet in English. It's only a mile wide but impossible to cross without being seen. To the right, however, is Hau Hoi Wan, or Deep Bay. Sham Chun river empties into it.

"It's a good deal wider and, despite the name, shallower. if you strike out across it you will come to the headland of Tsim Bei Tsui, which guards the extensive fish farms of Yuen Long. That's Hong Kong territory.

"This is what you do. Cycle out of here tonight. Go south-east about seventy miles, find Deep Bay and lie up for the day. Watch out for the guards in the border zone!

"The following evening, after it's dark, get down to the beach at dead of night, strip the inner tubes out of your bicycle tyres, inflate them and tie them together. They'll make a float for you.

"Then you swim out to the headland; it's less than four miles away. You're in luck, Peter; it'll be easy. You know why? There's a new moon and the weather should be overcast. That means it will be pitch black and the patrols won't spot you."

Peter looked dubious. "If it's that easy why doesn't everybody do it? And how do I know in which direction to swim in the pitch dark?"

"The answer to the first question is that quite a number of people have done it, but it does require stamina – and the ability to forget about the sharks. Remember, too, that the swimmers usually have friends or relations waiting for them with transport. Otherwise they get picked up by the local police for not having a Hong Kong identity card, after which they're promptly shunted back across the border.

"The answer to the second one is that a light will be visible on the headland for you to aim at."

"Sharks! Thanks very much! Who needs border patrols when they've got them? And what about this light on the headland? How do you know it will be shining tomorrow night?"

"Because, my lad, I shall be holding it! You need someone to meet you or you too will be picked up and deported. I was only kidding about the sharks; the fish in the bay are mostly mackerel and yellowtail.

"This is the plan. I go to Hong Kong tomorrow on the train. When I arrive I buy a powerful torch, with extra batteries, and a lens tinted amber to differentiate it from any others.

"Then I get hold of Pat and Tony, a couple I know, who own a small junk with an outboard motor; it happens to be lying at Yuen Long. I'm sure I can borrow it for a fishing expedition – they've lent it to me before.

"Fortunately I know those waters pretty well. I'll take the junk out through the fish farms and round the headland. I can anchor offshore somewhere between the village of Nam Sha Po and the Lau Fau Shan bird sanctuary. Then I'll put out a net, set up the torch like this, as a guiding light, and wait for you. How's that?"

Peter gazed at her with elated admiration. "You would do all that for a total stranger?" he said. "I don't know what to say. Gillian, you're wonderful – amazing! I shall owe you a lifelong debt. My guiding light!"

"Don't thank me yet. You're the one taking all the risks. I shall just be out for a night's fishing. Now I must go to bed. Goodnight, Peter, and good luck. Don't forget – aim for the amber light. And take care!"

He stood, clasped her hands fervently and strode from the room. Down in the hotel basement the thin, bespectacled Chinese clerk took off his headphones and lifted the cassette from his tape recorder.

He couldn't understand much of the conversation but the place names told him all he needed to know. Comrade Chang would be pleased with the tape. He could look forward to promotion in his cadre.

Next morning Chang was indeed pleased with the tape. He took it to his superior in the security service and they listened to it with satisfaction.

"So the *gwei-lo* (foreign devil) thinks he can get away, eh?" the commander mused grimly, switching off the tape recorder. "He is sadly mistaken, Chang, due to the vigilance of your staff. He will be apprehended."

"With respect, comrade," Chang said, "by now he is already in hiding near Hau Hoi Wan. That is a very large bay. Tonight the patrols will not find it easy to catch him. It will be very dark and they won't know at what point he will be entering the water."

"A good point, a very good point," replied the commander. "However there are more ways to skin a cat, as the Western devils say. We may not know where he is starting his swim but we do know where he intends to finish it. Somewhere off the headland of Tsim Bei Tsui, yes? A message to our comrades in the Hsin Hua news agency in Hong Kong should prove effective. Thank you, Chang, you may return to duty."

Gillian spent the day in some apprehension. She had outlined her plan to Peter confidently enough but now that she was in the train, on her way back to Hong Kong with the business delegation, some doubts occurred to her.

What if she couldn't find a suitable torch with an amber lens? What if Pat and Tony had lent their junk to someone else, or were using it themselves? She and Peter should have made contingency plans. Heroic choirs sang 'The East Is Red' over the train's loudspeakers while she stared out of the window at the endless rice paddies and worried at a fingernail.

In the event, however, all went well, to her great relief. Back in Hong Kong Tony agreed to lend her the little junk and by the time twilight descended she was puttering out to sea, net and new torch safely stowed. She followed the harbour lane between the fish farms and the Japanese oyster beds, turned to port and started to edge down the coast while there was still light in the sky.

After about half a mile she threw the motor into neutral and dropped anchor a hundred yards or so off the shore. She killed the motor and the junk rocked jauntily on the swell. Apart from the hushed sound of the surf the silence was as striking as it had been in Canton.

After sunset she eased the net overboard and settled down to wait for Peter, glancing back over her shoulder to check her position. To her astonishment the shoreline was not invisible in the blackness; it was lined by a long string of lights. They were not powerful lamps such as the fishermen used; they were more like torches – and they were all amber.

She puzzled over the sight for a few minutes until the explanation occurred to her. The Chinese security service must have discovered her plan in some way. Arrangements had been made for its sympathisers in Hong Kong to deploy a number of amber lights along the shore line, to confuse a swimmer looking for a particular one.

Such a swimmer would blunder ashore, into the arms of someone whose ruthlessness could be relied upon. Gillian set her jaw resolutely, got the torch out and turned back to the open sea. She must not let Peter down . . .

Marjorie turned the last page of the manuscript and found nothing more. Was that the end? Of course she knew that Peter had made it, since he and Gillian were right then sitting in the lounge listening to Radio Four. But how did it turn out? How did he find Gillian's guiding light among all the others? Or did he?

She jumped up and ran into the house. "Dad, I've read your story. It's tantalising! You stopped at the very point of success – or failure. Come on, tell me how you got away. You swam across that bay and found Mum, didn't you? How did you do it?"

Peter and Gillian looked at each other; Peter smiled. "Bit of a conjuring trick, wasn't it?" he said. "But the clue is right there, in the story. Remember what Gill said to me in that hotel room in Canton? She said, 'I'll put out a net and set up the torch *like this* as a guiding light.'

"When she said 'like this' she put one hand in front of the other and moved it up and down like a shutter. It was clear that the torch light would flash continuously. Our comrade listening in the basement couldn't guess that, since he had only the words on the tape to go on.

"When I swam across the bay on my inner tubes I saw a line of amber lights on the headland; they were very useful – they outlined it for me. But only one of them was flashing and that was the one I aimed for.

"Gill helped me climb into the junk soon after midnight. I was pretty tired but I was safe. My guiding light had saved me. That was the very first time we kissed." Gillian coloured.

"Nice one, Mum!" said Marjorie. "What an adventure! You were really cool. But there's one thing I still don't understand. Why couldn't you have told me the story years ago? Why the long silence?"

Peter and Gillian exchanged another look. Peter raised his eyebrows and tipped his head to one side. "Orders, I'm afraid.

"You see, by the time the Chinese guards took the camera off me in that village it had a different film in it. And that one really did have scenic views; I hope the security chaps had fun developing it.

"My own film went to GCHQ for processing. As a source of information it was, shall we say, more of a guiding light."

Caveat Vendor

MELINDA had never thought of herself as an introspective type. In fact she had never thought seriously about herself at all.

She was, she supposed, reasonably clear-thinking, moderately attractive and interested in food, clothes and the world around her. She was happy in her secretarial job and enjoyed weekends of tennis and reading. Questions of ethics didn't bother her – until, that is, she met Bernard, the archivist.

Superficially Bernard was an ideal counterpart. He was intelligent and articulate and, like Melinda, interested in what went on around him. He was good-looking, too, in an understated way, with his high forehead and direct, challenging expression. His steel-rimmed bifocals and old tweed coat reinforced the impression of a studious undergraduate on holiday.

Having been casual, but successful, partners on the tennis court she and Bernard found themselves drawn to each other. They liked the same friends, listened to the same kind of music and held a similar range of opinions. Melinda did not imagine for a moment that through Bernard she would be drawn into an ethical tangle – still less one that, even after all that happened, remained unresolved.

The affair began when Bernard arrived at the tennis club one day in a state of suppressed excitement. He ordered a couple of soft drinks and drew her to a table at the far end of the verandah, glancing round to make sure they could not be overheard.

"Look, Melinda," he said quietly, "this is going to sound highly suspicious, not to say alarming, but I need some money right away. I tried to borrow some from Tony, my flatmate, but he's as short as I am. So I thought I would ask you. I know, I know, it's a hell of a cheek but let me tell you the whole story.

"As you know I have a job with the local Council, in the archives department. Naturally I get to know quite a lot about the district both from records and from friends at work. Occasionally I help out with Social Services – elderly people who need shopping done, that sort of thing.

"Well, I've come across an old gentleman by the name of Naughton who is about to take a room in St Benedict's – that's the residential home in Parkside – and he needs to get rid of a few sticks of furniture and that kind of thing. He asked me if I could help him dispose of them – one in particular.

"Most of his stuff isn't remarkable – mid-thirties oak, that kind of thing – but that one piece is outstanding. It's a genuine highboy; you know what that is? A sort of tall chest of drawers with curlicue brass handles. It's real carved mahogany in superb condition with a scrolled pediment at the top, standing on cabriole legs. It seems to be eighteenth-century American, probably from Philadelphia."

"I'm impressed!" Melinda said. "I didn't know you were an expert on antiques."

"I'm not," Bernard smiled. "I got the description off Naughton. He knows that it's a fairly valuable piece and he's determined to get a good price for it. He's a rapacious old bird, that was my impression.

"But that wasn't the half of it. When I went to lift one corner, to see if I could get it down the stairs, I was surprised to find it was immensely heavy. I opened a couple of the drawers and found they were stuffed with papers of every size and colour.

"They were jammed in anyhow. Some were obviously letters and diaries but there were documents of all descriptions – thousands of them! I wasn't able to examine them closely with old Naughton wheezing away in his armchair, watching me, but I got enough of a look to give me a severe shock."

He leaned forward and lowered his voice still more. "To explain why, I have to take you back to eighteenth-century London. You've heard of Dr Johnson, haven't you? – Samuel Johnson who wrote *Lives of the Poets* and many other things but is best remembered now for his great *Dictionary of the English Language*? Bamber Gascoigne used to ask lots of questions about him on University Challenge, if you remember.

"Well, Johnson's fame rests largely on the efforts of a young Scots lawyer by the name of James Boswell, son of Lord Auchinleck. Boswell was what they used to call a 'coxcomb' in those days – a vain womaniser with a weakness for drink and stupefyingly garrulous.

"However he was a wonderful chronicler and his adulation for Johnson was genuine. As a result he left the world a biography of the great man which has become famous in itself.

"Now when Boswell died in 1795 his literary executors allowed his family to take charge of his huge collection of manuscripts. As nothing more was heard of them archivists like me assumed that all had been destroyed.

"This would have been understandable because the family had no wish to add to the fame of a man who, whatever his talents, had fathered an illegitimate child at the age of twenty-one. Furthermore he contracted venereal disease, engaged in numerous affairs (even while married) and, worst of all, wrote down all the details in his *London Journal*.

"But the papers had not been destroyed. In 1840 some of his letters were found by chance in Boulogne, of all places; they are now in the Pierpoint Morgan library.

"Much later the journal and some 4,000 other papers were located in Malahide Castle near Dublin; they're in Yale University. A professor from Aberdeen University found another hoard of manuscripts in Scotland and still more came to light at Malahide Castle during the War."

"It's like a treasure hunt!" Melinda said.

"That's right," Bernard went on. "However even now not all of Boswell's extraordinary collection has been found. Some of the letters he received from Rousseau and Voltaire, not to mention John Wilkes and Sir Joshua Reynolds, are missing. There must be others, too, from Corsica and the Hebrides and elsewhere. And there are certainly more diaries lying around somewhere."

He paused for breath while Melinda stared at him, wide-eyed. "So now you've discovered the missing items, is that it?" she said. "They're stuffed in this tallboy?"

"Highboy," he corrected. "Yes, I'm certain of it. I noticed that one of the letters was signed Isabella – that would be Isabella de Zuylen whom Boswell met in Utrecht. Any good archivist will tell you that."

"So what's the problem?" Melinda asked. "The old boy evidently doesn't want to keep the papers since he asked you to sell the cabinet. Surely he'll give you a commission if they're bought by Yale or that library you mentioned?"

"Maybe, maybe. But my belief is that he doesn't even know what they are! He told me that he was sorry to part with the highboy and wouldn't do so except that the room at St Benedict's was too small to accommodate it. He's willing for me to put it into a London auction. According to him it should fetch a good price."

"But nothing like the price the Boswell papers would fetch, I take it?"

"If they *are* the Boswell papers. Yes, they'd be worth a fortune, I should imagine. But I only got a glimpse of them – they might not be what I think they are. The best thing to do would be to examine them at leisure. That's why I need some money, to purchase the highboy and get hold of them."

Melinda was horrified. "Bernard, you can't do that! That's equivalent to stealing! The papers belong to him. He should be the one to receive money for them, if they're that valuable. It might mean he wouldn't have to go into St Benedict's after all."

"Hold on a tick! We don't know that the papers are his. Even if he is the true owner of the highboy the papers could belong to a relative or a friend – anyone!"

"That's a quibble and anyway the ownership is easy to establish. We'll just tell him what you think they are and he can say where they came from. You'll need to know that anyway if you're going to offer what-d'you-call-it, provenance, to the auction house."

Bernard smiled briefly. "For a secretary you're well up on auctions and things," he acknowledged. "But what about me? I'm not a thief, if you don't mind. If I were I'd simply remove the papers quietly before putting the cabinet up for auction. Of course I'd have to say how I came to have them and take the risk that old Naughton would find out. But in any case that's unthinkable.

"Neither am I a con artist, contrary to what you might be thinking. I have no intention of diddling the old boy. I am, however, a professional archivist. Aren't I entitled to a share of the proceeds?

"Remember, but for me old Naughton would never know the value of those papers – if they are what I think they are, that is.

Why shouldn't I buy them in a job lot, as it were? You might call it a case of Caveat Vendor – Let the Seller Beware!"

"I still say it's wrong," Melinda insisted, "and you know it, in your heart of hearts. It's a question of ethics, isn't it? Ethically speaking you should inform him of the estimated value of the papers and ethically he should reward you with a part of whatever he realises on them."

"That'll be the day!" Bernard muttered. "As I say, he's the grasping sort. If he suspects the true value of the papers he'll flog them to the highest bidder and grab the loot. I know it."

Melinda sat back to consider. "Whose ethics are the more reliable, I wonder? Yours or his? Quite a teasing problem. But one thing's for sure: you're going to have to move first since you're the one who knows the situation. What are you going to do?"

"Blimey, I don't know," said Bernard gloomily. "I don't want to deprive him of his just deserts but I get the feeling that he's not likely to share any of the proceeds with me. And if I let the highboy go as it is you can bet your bootees that whoever discovers the papers will be about as ethical as Niccolò Machiavelli."

Melinda stood up. "Come on, Bernard," she said. "Let's go and see this man Naughton. I'll speak to him on your behalf. I'm sure I can arrive at some arrangement that will be acceptable. And incidentally I don't have enough money to enable you to buy the highboy anyway, so we have no other course."

They left the club and Bernard drove her round to a small terraced house at the back of town. A plump cleaning woman answered the door and ushered them up to a room on the first floor. There a frail elderly man greeted Bernard from a chair near the gas fire.

"Ah, there you are, young man!" he said. "Come for the

Caveat Vendor

highboy, have you? Very good of you. Who's this? Your lady friend?"

Melinda stepped forward. "Hallo, Mr Naughton," she said. "I hope you don't mind my coming along with Bernard. He thought perhaps I could be of help."

"Ah, yes, I remembered what Bernard said about how difficult it was to get the cabinet down the stairs so I had Mrs Sutton take out all those old papers and put them on the bonfire. You'll find it's quite easy to handle now!"

No Offence Intended

LADIES and gentlemen of the jury! You have now heard the evidence presented in this case. You have had an opportunity to assess the witnesses and to weigh their testimony. In a few minutes you will hear counsel's final argument and his Lordship's summing up. Before that, however, I should like to say a few words.

The charge against the defendant, Michael Hannigan, is one of rape. Now, rape is an offence that inevitably arouses the emotions. The average person loathes such a crime; it is seen on a par with child abuse – worse, somehow, than a good clean robbery or swindle. Even those of a cynical turn of mind would have little mercy on a rapist.

You, ladies and gentlemen, will of course approach your deliberation impartially. You will be neither vindictive nor cynical. But because you are average people yourselves you will find that your feelings are engaged, whether you will it or not.

Let me very briefly review the facts. Mr Hannigan has told you that he had enjoyed an evening out with the girl he had been seeing for a couple of months. They had a meal and several drinks – maybe too many – before he escorted her home to her basement flat in Chelsea.

According to him she invited him in for a late-night coffee. He was happy to accept. They sat on the settee and she did not object when he kissed her with some ardour. One excitement led to another and they were about to "go all the way", as the colloquial phrase has it, when she suddenly drew back and pushed him away.

She said something shyly about scruples and also contraception but he brushed the remarks aside and grabbed her more tightly. He knew that she wanted him and he enjoyed making love to her although she seemed considerably less ardent that before. Afterwards, he says, he was shattered when she accused him of raping her.

As I said, this kind of story arouses feelings. Those of you who are men will have great difficulty, even in all sincerity, in gauging the effect of rape – its ghastly shock and subsequent trauma – because it is something that is very unlikely to happen to you. We understand that.

The women among you will have in-built attitudes to it, just as I have. These are derived from our home backgrounds and upbringing, our religion and perhaps our own sexual experiences. These things are inescapable.

I am not, of course, suggesting that you will be biased in one direction or another while considering this case. I am saying that there is inevitably a degree of moral judgement in all our minds when we contemplate the offence of rape. For that reason I should like to take a few minutes to consider the nature of this crime and hence the context in which you will be arriving at your verdict.

To do so I want to start from the most fundamental aspect of the law, of the application of which you, members of the jury, are now a part. I hope that you won't find it too remote and generalised. Please bear with me.

It is every governing body's obligation to promote and uphold law and order. In order to meet that obligation the government enacts laws and puts in place certain institutions to enforce them.

But although the laws of a civilised society are both numerous and complex – too numerous and complex, some people would say! – they all rest on one basic principle. That is the principle of protection.

You and I, ladies and gentlemen, enjoy protection in many different forms. We are, hopefully, protected against our enemies by the armed forces. We are protected against injury and disease by all sorts of hygiene and other regulations. And we look to the law for protection against fraud, theft, assault and murder.

When we come to the crime of rape we think principally of one kind of protection. Although rape may take place among any number of people of both sexes, especially in penal institutions or in time of war, we tend to think of it in one particular way, in the context of our society. We think of a man and a woman, alone.

Because a man is usually physically stronger than a woman our perception of this crime is that of 'him' compelling 'her' to engage in a sexual act, against her will and resistance. The typical image we have is of the lone woman walking home along a dark alley and a man leaping upon her from the shadows. Thus the man is the aggressor and the woman is the victim.

But although that stereotype may be true enough in a number of instances it is far from the truth in many others. In our modern community a considerable degree of equality had been achieved between the sexes. The fact that I, a woman, am addressing you in a court of law is a small illustration of that. I suggest, therefore, that it is time to question the application of the rape stereotype to every case of this kind that comes before a jury.

Let me be clear. I am not for one moment proposing to modify the legal definition of rape as a crime or the penalties attached to it. The man who leaps out of the alley shadows must be convicted and punished; we must be protected from him and all others like him. So that law must remain on the statute books.

No Offence Intended

However you, ladies and gentlemen, are men and women of the world. You know very well what makes that world go round, according to the saying. You know that men and women engage in sex principally as spouses but also as lovers and friends, to say nothing of commercial prostitution.

In these instances we normally presume that the two people concerned are willing partners, whether or not they are blissfully happy with the relationship. They are deemed to be 'consenting adults', to borrow a phrase from another type of relationship.

The trouble arises when one of them, typically the woman, does not consent. Then we may – and I emphasis *may* – have a case of rape. But not always. Remember the statistics: in the great majority of cases the rapist and the victim know each other well.

Let us look at an everyday situation. A young man meets a girl, is attracted by her and asks her to go out with him. She agrees and they become friends. Over several outings their feelings become warmer. They find pleasure in embraces and kisses.

One evening the man, confident that he is interpreting the girl's enthusiasm correctly, takes advantage of a secluded situation. His caresses become more intimate. The girl initially appears to respond.

What happens next we do not know. It is a feature to be expected in any crime, but most especially rape, that no witnesses will be available. That is why many women in the past failed to complain. They knew that it would be their word against the man's and they feared that they would be branded as vindictive perjurers, encouraging a man's advances while denying such encouragement later.

These days women are less reticent, thank goodness. But in any legal proceedings a jury like you will still have to rely mainly on what is known as circumstantial evidence. No one is going to

No Strings Attached

help you by appearing in the witness box and swearing that they saw the act committed.

So how we do become aware of a possible offence? After the alleged incident the girl will probably appear distressed. She will accuse the man of ignoring her protests and overcoming her frantic efforts to deter him. She may go so far as to support a prosecution for rape.

It is not difficult, of course, to prove that intercourse took place. A medical examination can establish that, if the girl can overcome her reluctance to consult a doctor without delay. But here we are not concerned with the occurrence *per se*. We are trying to establish whether she consented to it. And that is vastly more difficult.

What we are dealing with is something to which the Americans, in their inventiveness, have given a label. As you may know, they call it 'date rape'. The label means that the girl and the man are in an accepted dating relationship, seeking to be alone and enjoying the kisses and caresses of a loving couple. Then the man goes further than the girl intended.

So what is our view? This brings us back to the point I was making at the outset. The view we take is surely affected by our moral judgement. Those of us, probably men, who are urbane and hard-headed will tend to dismiss the allegations.

They acknowledge that a man should remain a gentleman at all times. However they will ask what on earth the girl was doing in such an intimate setting, if she was not at least ready to contemplate a sexual relationship. They may go further and question whether a girl who goes into such a situation can reasonably call upon the protection of the law if she changes her mind at the last moment?

Others, more probably women, will be uncompromising. Rape, even more than any other act against the will of someone else, is immoral and must be penalised. Otherwise no woman is safe. Is a girl to be deprived of the protection of the law just because she exchanges some cuddles and kisses with a man she knows well? Surely not. For them there is no mitigation.

The men, of course, can turn that argument to their own purposes. They will ask, in turn, how any man can ask a girl out on a date in the ordinary way, and be alone with her, if the possibility exists that she will later accuse him of rape. Just what is a man supposed to do if the girl suddenly says 'no' in the middle of the proceedings? Hence who is to say if what he does is in fact legal or not?

In the world outside this courtroom it comes down to a matter of probabilities. Was her refusal clear? Is it likely, in other words, that a rape did take place? But the law requires you to be sure 'beyond reasonable doubt' of the defendant's guilt before you pronounce him guilty. To be judged guilty 'on the balance of probability', as in a disciplinary hearing, is not enough.

Obviously this is something of a minefield. And yet, members of the jury, there is a way out. We can find it by looking at the case of Mike Tyson, the boxer, in the United States. Tyson, you will remember, was convicted of raping a participant in a beauty contest. She had accompanied him to his hotel room after midnight and given him reason to think that she welcomed his attentions.

But he was convicted of rape. Why? Because that jury had no latitude. Either a crime had been committed or it hadn't. Since the circumstantial evidence showed that sexual intercourse had taken place they had to say that Tyson behaved in the same way as the archetypal man springing out of the shadows in the alley.

Clearly the two situations were totally different. Yet the man enjoying coition in the hotel room was found guilty of rape, just as the alley attacker would have been.

The fault, you see, lies in the law. The law says that rape is 'unlawful carnal knowledge' procured by fear, force or fraud. It does not specify whether the act occurs in an alleyway or a hotel room. In fact it says nothing at all about the relationship between the man and the woman, or the circumstances surrounding that relationship.

What is needed, I suggest, is another category of offence – a category that I may call, for the purpose of discussion, a sexual assault.

That lesser category would cover the 'date rape' types of occurrence. It would enable a jury to bring in a guilty verdict in such a case without fearing that the defendant would be sentenced to a long period of imprisonment. And it would still leave the crime of rape, meaning unprovoked sexual attack, on the statute book for the protection of women.

Such a change in the law is long overdue. I hope very much that I have been able to show you that. But of course even if you agree with me you will no doubt be wondering how all this is relevant. You will be obliged to apply the law as it stands, not as it might be in an ideal world. I'm sure his Lordship will say something to you along those lines when he invites you to consider your verdict.

So, ladies and gentlemen, my appeal is to your moral judgment. As you know, the jury in the first trial of this case failed to agree. We do not know how their deliberations went, nor should we know. But I would dare hazard a guess that if they had been able to exercise their moral judgement they would have achieved unanimity.

This time I have chosen to conduct my own case. What Michael Hannigan did to me in my basement flat was shameful and repugnant. It forfeited my esteem for him and damaged my relationship with any future boyfriend. I shall not feel completely secure, when alone with a man, for some time to come.

But thank goodness I have suffered no lasting harm. I am not promiscuous but I have to say that I was – well, I wasn't a virgin when I met Michael.

What he did was wrong. It was a sexual assault. I am not asking for a Not Guilty verdict but for mercy. I have watched him suffer during two trials and the period in between. That has been his punishment.

In my heart I have forgiven Michael. I now ask you to do the same. Thank you.

The Customer's Not Always Right

SYLVIA stirred her cup of tea abstractedly. From her table in the alcove she had a good view of the little café, now starting to fill up with lunch-time customers.

For the centre of a small market town the café was surprisingly unpretentious. The furniture was solid and unremarkable, the walls appeared to have been painted a dull green over the original wallpaper and the fluorescent lights gleamed from no-nonsense fittings.

It was a typical family-run business, Sylvia decided. It confirmed what she had thought on peering at the sun-curled menu through the window before she entered. Not knowing the town she had had to make a quick assessment; this place seemed to suit her purposes admirably.

"So you want to become a social worker?" her mother had said the previous evening. "Not a popular line at the moment, I believe. Once upon a time they were tolerated – all the questions, the intrusiveness and so on. Now, people are beginning to doubt their judgement."

"I'm not talking about child abuse or adoption decisions," Sylvia said. "I just want to work among people who need help. Counselling, I suppose you'd call it."

"For that you need to be a psychologist," her mother stated

flatly. "You know what psychology is? Common sense with Latin names added. And you know how to acquire common sense? Observation! You have to watch people – all kinds of people – to see what makes them tick. Because you'll get all sorts. You know the old saying: You live long enough, you meet 'em all!"

Sylvia had been sufficiently impressed by this robust opinion to start her observation course right away. Her job in the insurance office was not inspiring and as it was Saturday there was time to look around.

She decided that she couldn't hover in a public place to watch people in her own locality – there was too much chance of bumping into acquaintances – so she slipped a notebook into her shopping bag, took a bus to a nearby town and set out to observe. The little café offered both refreshment and opportunity.

At the 'ting' of the doorbell she looked up. A family entered, a plump careworn woman in the lead followed by a beefy man with ginger hair and a moustache and two boys, tall teenagers in faded jeans.

They looked about for a moment and then made for a table close to Sylvia's. She noticed that as they sat down they didn't say anything to each other; the only sounds were of chairs scraping back and plastic menus being slapped on the table top.

After a minute or two a young waitress appeared through the kitchen swing door, scooped up some knives and forks and a bottle of ketchup from a side table and came over to the newcomers. She smiled briefly as she leaned between them to arrange the cruet, cutlery and paper napkins.

"About time," the beefy man muttered. "Now then, we haven't got much time. We want cod and chips all round, young lady. Like it says here, under Fish – four pounds, service included. That's twelve quid altogether, right? And no extras added on, thank you."

The waitress hesitated, flustered. "Four cod and chips? I think you'll find that's sixteen pounds, sir," she suggested.

"No, no, twelve," the man insisted. "Look, it says here 'Children half-price on weekdays'. Kevin and Stephen are children. That's two fours and two twos, twelve pounds, all right? And get a move on, if you don't mind; we've got a bus to catch."

The young waitress gulped nervously and seemed to tighten her grip on the bottle of ketchup. "I'm sorry, sir. As it says, the half-price is on weekdays. This is a weekend, you see."

"What? What do you mean, a weekend? This isn't a Sunday, is it? If it's not a Sunday it's a weekday. I should have thought that was obvious. So it's half-price for the kids. As advertised." The beefy man closed the menu, sat back and folded his arms, chin up.

The waitress looked stricken. She opened her mouth, glanced at the beefy man and closed it again before scurrying away to the swing door. As before, the family sat in silence, eyes on the table top apart from the beefy man. Sylvia began to reach for her notebook but the thought that he might notice stopped her.

The kitchen door swung again and a stocky man strode through with a purposeful air. His hair was also somewhat gingery and, given the difference in age, his face was not unlike the beefy man's in its square lines and set expression. He approached the family table and rested his hands on a chair back.

"Good morning, sir. I'm the manager. Sorry if there's a misunderstanding. On fish and chips we make a special offer of half-price to children on weekdays – that's Monday to Friday – but that doesn't include weekends, I'm afraid."

The beefy man bridled. "Your menu says half-price on weekdays. This is a weekday, isn't it? It's not a Sunday. So let's have the kids' meals at the price on the menu and no argy-bargy, all right?"

The manager straightened up and fiddled with a coat button.

The Customer's Not Always Right

"As I've explained, sir, the offer is intended to apply Monday to Friday only. However we needn't labour the point because the half-price is for children. These lads are hardly children, are they? How old are you, son?"

"Don't cross-question my kids!" snapped the beefy man. "You can see they're not adults, can't you? Therefore they're children, right? And as such they're entitled to half-price meals. Now let's get on with it. Or do you want me to get in touch with the trading standards officer?"

Sylvia swallowed in excitement. Her observational field trip was certainly paying off. She glanced at the wife who was sitting facing her, expressionless. Clearly she wasn't going to intervene and neither man was going to back down.

Sylvia wondered what she herself would do in the circumstances. She remembered a bit of psychology jargon. Would her 'communication skills', whatever they were, come to her aid in a situation like this?

Maybe the half-price offer was loosely worded but the ginger-haired man seemed determined to be as unreasonable as possible. Hoping that the two wouldn't come to blows she watched as the manager bent forward again.

"Please, sir. Let's not get this out of proportion. We are a catering establishment offering a service to whomever we wish at reasonable prices. The trading standards officer knows that. Now, if you would like four portions of fish and chips we shall be happy to supply them to you, at the usual price."

The beefy man lifted his chin still further and peered balefully at the manager. "It says half-price on weekdays and that's what I want," he said heavily. "If you're not prepared to serve the boys at that price they can go without. We'll have two portions, thank you, for me and the missus. That'll be eight pounds. So you've lost out, haven't you?"

"The two lads are having nothing at all, is that it?" asked the manager.

"That's right. If they can't have what's on the menu they don't want anything. To hell with it!"

The manager's expression hardened. "In that case, sir, I should be grateful if they would vacate their seats so that we can serve other customers. This is our busy period just now. I'm sure you understand."

"Vacate their seats? Talk English, man! You want them to get up! They're not allowed to sit with us while we have lunch, is that it? What kind of place is this, anyway? Where a family can't sit together to have a snack?"

"This is a restaurant, sir, not an airport lounge. Seats are provided for those ordering meals. The arrangement is perfectly normal in every way."

"Normal, is it?" the beefy man responded. "Right! You want the letter of the law, you can have it. Get up, you two, and wait till we're ready." He turned back to the manager. "I hope you're satisfied at last?"

Sylvia couldn't believe her eyes. The table now had the appearance of a photographer's studio, with the beefy man and his wife still seated impassively, the two tall teenagers standing like sentries over the empty chairs and the manager and young waitress in agonised attitudes in the background.

It was evident that the cod and chips was not going to arrive and equally obvious that no other couple was going to take the chairs while the two lads towered over them. It was a complete impasse.

She took out her notebook and opened it. This was what psychology students called a case study, she thought. She began to scribble a few words when a second thought came to her.

Observation was all very well but she didn't want to be a

The Customer's Not Always Right

journalist, after all; she wanted to be a counsellor. Wouldn't it be more relevant, and much more helpful, to try to resolve the situation rather than merely record it?

Sylvia put the notebook away, summoned up her resolve and went over to the still-life group. "Excuse me," she said tentatively, "I couldn't help overhearing. Could I be of any assistance? I might be able to help reach some kind of compromise."

To her astonishment the beefy man and the café manager looked at each other and burst out laughing; the woman and the two boys joined in.

"Something like ACAS, you mean?" chuckled the man. "That's very sweet of you, love, but you don't understand." He pointed to the manager. "This is Bob, my oldest boy. He's going to be running my café while the wife and I have a few weeks' holiday. Eventually he'll be taking over completely.

"I just wanted to make sure that in addition to the cooking and general management he was able to cope with the people who come in off the street. You have to be a diplomat in this trade, you know. So I arranged to give him a little test. What did you think of it? I call it The Customer Isn't Always Right!"

A Better Proposal

WHEN Catherine opened her eyes in the early morning sunlight she immediately felt that something was not right. She lay in bed with her face turned towards the window and tried to identify the source of her unease.

The buttercup-yellow curtains moved gently in the summer breeze, throwing their usual faint glow of reflected light over the black lacquer bowl on the window sill. From out in the road come the reassuring rising whine of Charlie's milk-float as it moved off to his next call. The familiar fragrance of Aunt Mary's dried herbs came to her as she rubbed her cheek into the pillow.

Everything seemed comfortingly normal in this little seaside town. Nothing was out of place. The coming day, too, presented no fears or challenges. After the household chores she had only a certain amount of tidying up to do in the workshop before departing for the theatre in the evening. What was this cloud of melancholy hovering over her?

She sat up and, as though a torch beam had been switched on, she recognised her mood. It was one of disappointment. And the disappointment, of course, came from what had happened the previous evening – or rather, what had not happened.

Catherine ran over the scene in her mind, as she had done over and over before falling asleep some time after midnight. Earlier on, at about half-past nine, all had seemed propitious. She had made her preparations with care. The scene in which her protagonists, as she thought of them, were to meet was meticulously arranged.

The drawing-room was cheerful with flowers and well lit. The sofa had been coaxed into a central position and was flanked by low tables bearing books and a small lamp. A trolley stood nearby with glasses, a tray of coffee and a shiny box of chocolates on the lower shelf.

Catherine had seen to it that Irene was the first to arrive. She remembered how Irene had crossed the room with that languid gait of hers and had taken up a position near the sofa, almost as if posing for an invisible sculptor. Irene's face betrayed no hint of either pleasure or apprehension as she stood there.

Henry came in shortly afterwards. In contrast he walked rather stiffly and hesitantly, Catherine thought, as he approached the trolley and made a gesture of offering Irene a drink. Catherine was too far off to hear what the two of them said to each other but that didn't matter. She had brought them together, in the right setting; surely things would take their course.

For a while that indeed seemed to be the case. Henry and Irene turned towards each other, appeared to bow pleasantly, admired the room, looked at each other again and eventually sat together on the sofa.

They sipped their drinks and put them down. Henry took Irene's hand and drew her close. They were clearly in earnest conversation, so intimate that Catherine could hardly wait for Henry to go down on one knee in the time-honoured manner. She clasped her hands together in anticipation.

But it came upon her, quite suddenly and blackly, that something was jarringly wrong. These two on the sofa did not look like lovers, somehow. In fact they looked as if they had scarcely been introduced, let alone been enjoying each other's company for some time. Irene, in particular, gave an impression of bored detachment, as though the conversation had been rehearsed a dozen times, to the point of meaninglessness.

Catherine could not bear to watch any longer. The encounter was giving her no pleasure, anyway. She turned away, distressed that her fond well-intentioned plans were apparently coming to nothing. Maybe Henry and Irene weren't the ideal couple after all.

She had stumbled out into the road and had set off at a brisk pace along the seafront, heading nowhere in particular. Her mind ranged over the past weeks as she wondered if she had made a grave mistake and, if so, where. Could she have been completely wrong about this young pair?

When Henry had made his first appearance he was a trifle rough and uncouth. His clothes seemed to hang askew on his angular frame and his movements were abrupt and awkward. But gradually, under Catherine's influence, he had developed some urbanity. His presence was more assured and he even acquired a degree of polished charm.

Catherine recalled, with a twinge of embarrassment, that she had been somewhat drawn to him herself, to the extent of giving him a chaste kiss on his cheek at the close of one companionable evening.

Irene, on the other hand, required no polishing. From the beginning she showed the calm repose of the well-bred girl. Her clothes were fresh and dainty, her hair had not a strand out of place and her attitude suggested a warm and personal interest in everyone and everything about her. How could she and Henry fail to hit it off?

Catherine sighed and glanced out to sea before turning back home. As she did so she caught a glimpse of a dark shape moving though the waves in the moonlight.

It wouldn't have been a shark's fin or anything like that, of course, but occasionally the head of an inquisitive seal could be seen from the promenade. Maybe, she thought, the resort could acquire its own dolphin, like that other place up north. She trudged home and went to bed.

Now, on this sunny morning, Catherine had a flash of inspiration. She threw back the bedclothes and crossed to her dressing table to study her face. It was the thought of the dolphin that had led to her excited discovery.

What was it about dolphins that so endeared them to human beings? Not their intelligence or their ability to perform entertaining tricks, for these were characteristics shared by several other animals. No, it was their human expression – that upturned corner of a permanent disarming smile, hinting at a secret chuckle, that was so attractive. A dolphin smiled, come what may.

And now she knew exactly what had disappointed her so keenly about Henry and Irene. They never smiled. No matter how close they were, no matter how strong their affection, their faces remained blank – blank and disappointing.

Catherine tried smiling at herself in the mirror. Yes, it worked! She knew now, with certainty, what she had to do.

She washed quickly, flung her clothes on and rushed to the workshop. Irene and Henry lay in their velvet-lined case, staring blank-faced as always. She took the puppets up, one by one, and with a few deft strokes of craft knife and paint brush brought warm tender looks to their wooden features.

Catherine relaxed with a little sigh of satisfaction. She need no longer fear the cramped lighting box at the rear of the theatre. In that evening's performance the betrothal scene would carry complete conviction.

Present and Correct

WHEN Maureen turned to put the roll of sticky tape away she saw the cardboard shape with its hump of clear plastic lying innocently on the table. She made a face at it. It was a pack of four small batteries and she had forgotten to enclose it in her parcel. Batteries Not Included even in the spirit of generosity, she thought. That would have been a good start to Christmas Day for a little girl.

With a small puff of exasperation she unwrapped the box again, pressing the paper flat to get rid of the new creases, and contemplated a fresh difficulty. If she put the battery pack alongside the box it would create an unsightly lump when she drew the paper tight again. That would be a pity because the wrapping paper featured a very large and jolly Santa riding on a sleigh with reindeer, gnomes and robins in profusion. It had to be seen flat for the full effect.

On the other hand if she broke the seals on the box and popped the batteries inside it might look as if the present was not brand-new. That would not worry the excited girl but it would certainly interest her mother. She might even express her disapproval.

Maureen dropped onto a stool and considered the problem. She didn't have much time. From a loudspeaker up in the corner of the room a sleek-voiced choir sang We Three Kings From OrienTar yet again. Tar very much, she thought. It's all right for you lot; you got your Christmas wrapped up months ago, in a distant recording studio.

She remembered the time, years ago, when she was roped into a choir. It wasn't a proper choir with tenors and altos and everything; just a group of children with a few young mothers. They called themselves the Knock-Out Choir "because we're a lot of bantam waits" as one mum said. Maureen hadn't understood but she liked the name.

The Knock-Out Choir toured the neighbourhood tossing snowballs at each other, singing lustily on doorsteps and collecting mince pies until the makeshift lantern caught fire and had to be doused in the snow. One householder gave them a parcel, she remembered. It was poorly wrapped in crumpled brown paper and the string came off.

They carried it back carefully to her house to open it ceremonially on the kitchen table. Inside there were sweets and mandarin oranges for the bantam waits, which cheered them up before they all went home. But the occasion wasn't very exciting. That was when Maureen realised the importance of wrapping a present correctly.

Her mother, wise and loving, had told her about selecting a present. You didn't choose something you wanted or something that attracted you in a shop window. You started by thinking of the person you were giving to – what sort of things they liked and the kind of thing they might not have already. And you didn't worry too much about the price – not in order to avoid extravagance but because the price mattered less than the suitability of the gift.

It was all good and valuable advice but there was one additional requirement, she realised. The present had to be done up correctly. The wrapping must be eye-catching, even opulent. It must conceal the shape of the contents and it must be secured in such a way that it took some little time to tear open. That increased the sense of expectancy and also the element of surprise.

Maureen stared at the revealed box in front of her and wondered for the umpteenth time if the contents would appeal to Emily. It was not the sort of thing she would have wanted at little Emily's age but it was a different world now. Everyone, boys and girls, played with electronic gadgets of fearsome complexity. In fact it wasn't so much a question of today's world, she reflected; it was more tomorrow's world.

Her mother's advice came back to her. It didn't matter whether she herself would like the Game That Thinks in the box. The question was, would Emily play with such a game as much as Maureen had played with her dolls? Suitable for ages 6–14, it said on the box. That ought to be all right but Maureen still wasn't sure.

Emily was her niece and Maureen didn't want her sister complaining that she had turned her daughter into a games addict or, even worse, an arcade loiterer. On the other hand if she gave Emily a set of hairbrushes or a jigsaw it might look like a return to Victorian values. Her sister was not a Women's Lib pioneer but she certainly believed in equality and was not backward in voicing her opinions.

Maureen came heavily to a decision. She stripped the batteries out of the pack and taped them to one end of the box so they lay flat. Then she re-wrapped it, smoothing jolly Santa flat and making knife-edge creases where the ends of the paper folded over.

She picked up her scissors, took a reel of silver ribbon and curled a length of it into a pom-pom like a chrysanthemum head. Sticking it down carefully near one corner, she picked up the parcel and took it through the swing door behind her.

"There we are, madam!" she said to the slim young woman at

the counter. "And thank you for using our gift-wrap service. I'm sure your daughter will enjoy opening her present."

Then she went off to the toy shelf to get another one – with batteries – for Emily.

The Ferry Game

Before she visited Bermuda Gillian had never heard of the ferry game. All she wanted was an exotic holiday.

She was attracted by brochure pictures of pink and white houses set among oleander bushes, to say nothing of sun-scorched coral beaches complete with waving palms, and decided to take a mid-Atlantic break. It was to be a two-week rest-cure with sun-tan. But that was before she became entangled in the ferry game.

It all began with Michael Denyer and his glum expression. A very endearing glum expression.

She first bumped into him when she was delivered by the airport taxi to her guest house, swathed in hibiscus blossom. She found that it commanded a splendid view of the harbour, as advertised, and had a path of crunchy gravel down to the beach.

To reach the town of Hamilton, however, one had to walk down to Queenskettle pier and take a ferry. The alternative was a long autocycle ride round the head of the harbour, a hot and humid experience.

Michael, she learned, was staying at the guest house while he waited for his own bungalow to be refurbished. On weekdays, like many other residents, he took the early ferry across the water to his office in Hamilton and returned the same way in the evening.

When Gillian saw him on the guest house verandah the following morning he was gazing out over the twinkling blue water with that quizzically glum expression while stirring his breakfast coffee abstractedly. Apart from that he was rather attractive in his off-white shirt and Bermuda shorts, with his keen blue eyes and sandy hair.

When they got into conversation over drinks a couple of days later Gillian felt bold enough to ask him what it was that had seemed to be causing him frustration.

"Was it that obvious?" he smiled. "Well, to tell the truth I was thinking about the ferry game – or rather what was being done to the ferry game."

"The ferry game?" she prompted.

"Sorry, I forgot you didn't know. The ferry game is a little competition that we, the commuters, take part in every morning. Harmless enough, you might think. But recently it's caused quite a furore among the players; in fact it's becoming a full-blown scandal."

Gillian pushed her sunglasses over the top of her head and leaned on one elbow. "Sounds intriguing!" she said. "Tell me more."

"Well, let's see now. Where shall I begin? I think it all started when the ferry company put a new and bigger boat on the cross-harbour run. I expect you've noticed that a number of residents like myself who live in Warwick and Paget parishes commute to and fro across the harbour. Most of us know each other in the same way as regular commuters do on suburban trains.

"Under the new timetable the first passenger ferry leaves Queenskettle at seven fifteen in the morning. The passengers are workers in Hamilton – there aren't many tourists at that hour.

"In this warm climate it's quite pleasant waiting for the ferry to dock in the early sunshine. People take their *Mid-Ocean News* and read it while waiting; there are plenty of seats among the 'wait-a-bit' bushes."

He passed one hand over a perspiring forehead and took a pull at a tall frosted glass of rum punch.

"Well," he went on, "somebody or other noticed that the ferry arrived at a different time each morning. It seemed that the boat was moored round that point there overnight and was brought to the jetty for the first run at about seven o'clock. But because of the vagaries of the tide and the wind and so on it sometimes came in well before seven and sometimes a good deal later, only just in time for the 7.15 departure.

"Eventually old Doc Trimingham thought up a little game to enliven the journey. He started to take bets on when the ferry would touch the quay – to the nearest half-minute. Winner to take all the stakes.

"Somehow the thing caught on and he equipped himself with a clipboard and a receipt book. Most of us played, at 70p or a dollar a go, and with getting on for a hundred passengers participating the prize soon became well worth winning."

"Sounds fairly innocuous," Gillian commented. "Where does the glumness factor come in?"

"Ah, that comes in – or came in – along with Charlie Bunnous. I don't know where he lives but I've seen him behind the counter at the Piggly-Wiggly store. Short fellow with a domed forehead and cheap round glasses.

"He started to play the game along with the rest of us but after a week or so it became apparent to everyone that he was winning – and I mean winning consistently. When he'd pocketed his fifth or sixth kitty in a row questions began to be asked.

"The chaps didn't mind losing, you understand. They were quite prepared to contribute their dollar a day if they could look forward to winning a spot of cash, say once a quarter. But they weren't at all happy seeing all the lolly going to a newcomer day after day, with few others getting a look-in.

The Ferry Game

"Some unkind remarks were made about jammy so-and-so's with 'second sight'. In the end a group of them came to me and asked me if I could look into the matter."

"Why you?" Gillian enquired.

"I should have mentioned – I'm a detective with the local force, on loan from the Yard. It's a six-month training stint so they're giving me a bungalow – better than a hotel room. The commuters probably asked me to do something because I'm not local.

"Anyway, I wasn't too keen at first. I mean, I'm here to train, not to investigate. And after all, if Charlie did have the luck of the Irish what was I supposed to do about it?

"It would be puerile to wind the game up just because a certain player won too many times. Equally, I could hardly go to Charlie and ask him not to play any more, while we went on playing. What possible reason could I give?

"But after a day or two I became fascinated by the problem. I worked out the probability that one player could predict the arrival time of the ferry so consistently as to win everybody's money and found that the odds against it were astronomical.

"So I came to the same conclusion as the others. He couldn't be genuinely successful. Some sort of fiddle was going on, I was convinced of it. But what could it be and how did it work?

"I decided to check on Charlie's movements as far as I could without alerting him. The following evening I spotted him on the hillside near here with binoculars and a torch. He wasn't doing anything much, just admiring the view and possibly bird-watching. Presumably the torch was to help him return home if darkness caught up with him.

"And that was that. The Great Detective was stuck! Charlie works all day in his store and takes an occasional nature walk in the evening. But somehow he knows to the minute – to the half-minute, in fact – when the ferry is going to come in the following morning. And makes a lot of money from that knowledge. I think I need a fresh mind on the problem. Any ideas?"

Gillian broke off a sprig of bougainvillaea at the corner of the verandah and tried the purple colour against her blouse; it looked quite striking. She thought for a moment.

"Tell me exactly how this ferry game is played," she said. "Is there some way in which he can make his entry after he learns the arrival time?"

"I don't see how," Michael replied. "What happens is that Doc Trimingham goes round on the return run every evening asking people to guess the arrival time of the ferry the next morning. He writes the guesses down on his clipboard and nobody sees it again until next day when he pins up the carbon undercopy on the notice board on Hamilton quay, and it turns out that Charlie has got it right yet again."

"I hesitate to suggest it," Gillian went on, "but is it possible that your Doc Whatsisname is in cahoots with Charlie? Perhaps he writes in Charlie's entry when the winning time is known?"

"Unthinkable!" Michael said. "Doc Trimingham is what you call a pillar of the community. He comes from one of the island's oldest families and, as I say, is a pillar of rectitude.

"Furthermore, a few weeks back he was off sick for a couple of days and another chap, the manager of the Bank of Butterfield, took over. It didn't make any difference. Charlie won the next day, as usual."

Gillian made a little sound in her throat. "And he wins every time, does he?"

"Not quite every time," Michael conceded, "but about two out of three, I would say. Enough to raise the deepest suspicions, anyhow."

"I see," she said. "Well, leave it with me, as they say. I'm not promising anything but if something occurs to me I'll let you know. Thanks for the drink. Good night!"

Over the next couple of days Gillian pondered on the winning ways of Mr Bunnous. Could he perhaps work out, from the state of the tide and the radio weather forecast, that the ferry would be delayed on its way to the jetty? Even if he could, how would he be able to get the time right when the boat was unusually early? Maybe it could be delayed leaving its berth in some way that he was aware of in advance?

While she was pondering the mystery she took the opportunity to travel on the early ferry, avoiding Michael's eye. She saw Doc Trimingham taking the passengers' bets and even had a guess herself. Nothing seemed to be amiss in any way.

When the ferry arrived at Hamilton it docked next to a large freighter. Stepping down onto the quay Gillian was astonished to see a small elephant being hoisted ashore in broad slings. It had its trunk in its mouth as a precaution against injury and its little eyes seemed wide with fright. A deck hand informed her that a circus was visiting the island and the animals would be there for only a week.

She went on to poke about among the commercial shipping, chatting to container depot staff and old salts on the fishing smacks. She learned little about the cross-harbour ferries. In fact there didn't seem to be any abnormalities in port operations that could account for variable arrival times.

Her own guess for a dollar was not a winner but she and Michael enjoyed the weekend together. They visited the stocks in St George's, toured a perfume factory and went swimming together.

On the Monday Michael went back to work while Gillian gravitated to Elba Beach and stretched out in the sun. She lay on her beach towel in what she hoped was an attractive pose and puzzled over the situation while the glare from the coral tanned the underneath of her chin.

She was nearing the end of her holiday and the solution to the mystery still eluded her. That was aggravating. It would have been pleasant to give Michael a small success to report to his colleagues before returning to London.

Gillian knew nothing about detective work. In fact, she had only come across a real-life detective once before. That was the time when a genial quiet-spoken man had come to her school to investigate a break-in. He had asked some of the girls a few questions and then departed. She never knew if the culprit was caught.

She remembered the detective being introduced to them all at school assembly by old Prosser in his tattered gown. Pross was the oldest member of the teaching staff, probably past retiring age if the truth were known, and his eccentricities were something of a school tradition.

Pross used to say that there was no such thing as an insoluble problem. First you had to make sure that you had all the information necessary to find the solution and secondly you had to look at the problem from all conceivable angles. Voila! That was all there was to it.

Gillian assembled the information about the ferry game in her mind and doggedly went over all the angles. It was no good. She snoozed, with memories of old Pross and the circus elephant mingling in her mind.

Suddenly she sat up, nearly crying out when the method suddenly worked. Of course! That was how Charlie got his winning times. From his point of view it was simple and it was just about foolproof, like all the best stratagems. But, as old Prosser had maintained, the problem wasn't insoluble.

She stood, brushed off some crumbs of coral and strode back

The Ferry Game

to the guest house. What was the best way to exploit her knowledge? She thought of dumping the problem on Michael Denyer but hesitated.

Since she had no proof and as the wily Charlie would continue to commute with the others she really needed to stop him working his ingenious trick without exposing him publicly. After a few moment' thought she sat down and wrote a short note addressed to Mr Bunnous and sealed it into an envelope.

That evening she gave the envelope to Michael and told him to pass it on to Charlie. Michael gave her a searching look but he said nothing.

The following evening, though, he was both articulate and ecstatic. "Gill, you're brill!" he said, whirling her round in a pirouette. "You did the trick!

"Charlie donated half of his winnings to the ferry game fund and undertook not to play the game any more. Amazing! Come on, tell me what you wrote in that note I gave him. Whatever it was, it was magic!"

Gillian looked down modestly. "I hadn't intended to give him away," she said, "but as he gave back only half the winnings maybe I'd better tell you.

"While I was sunbathing I started to think about how a trick like Charlie's could be worked; I remembered one of our teachers insisting that any problem could be solved, given sufficient information. He was an old traditionalist, a real Mr Chips. And that's what gave me the answer. Mr Chips and circus animals – horses, to be precise."

Michael goggled at her. "Chips – circus horses? What in creation are you on about?" he said. "What have chips and horses got to do with it?"

"Hush, and I'll tell you," Gillian replied. "Old Prosser – that was our Mr Chips – had one or two mannerisms and habits in which he took delight. One of them was to take his place at morning assembly while the school bell was ringing.

"He timed his slow shuffle so exactly that he reached his chair just as the bell stopped. At that very moment! He was never too early or too late. As the last 'dong' of the bell sounded he sat down. The school used to hold its breath, wondering if one day he would get it wrong, but he never did. Now, how do you think he did that?"

Michael shook his head. "I've no idea. How did he manage it?"

"Like all good tricks it was very simple," Gillian said. "It all depended on how you looked at it. You see, he didn't really sit down just as the bell stopped; what happened was that the bell stopped just as he sat down."

"So? What's the difference?"

"The difference is vital," said Gillian. "In reality the school porter, who was ringing the bell, was anxious to preserve Prosser's reputation for precision and detail. So he watched and made sure that when the old boy sat down the bell stopped. The thing wasn't prearranged but of course Pross cottoned on and played up to it.

"It was a harmless conceit for the old chap. But it set me thinking. If such a performance were arranged in advance the onlookers could be deceived. And that's exactly what was happening with your ferry game.

"When Charlie predicted the time at which the ferry would arrive the following morning he didn't need to know the answer. He just wrote down any reasonable time and left it to the captain to manoeuvre the ferry so that it arrived at the time specified.

"Of course he was in league with the captain. He had to be. He probably signalled the winning time to the ferry after its last run the previous day with that torch that you noticed. It was that simple."

The Ferry Game

Michael Denyer bowed. "Magnificent!" he breathed. "That had us all stumped but you got it. Well done, indeed. Would a champagne dinner be acceptable?"

"Any time!" Gillian laughed. "Now you know what I wrote in the note. Incidentally, since he doubtless had to give half his winnings to the ferry captain you ought to get on to *him* as well. Threaten him with exposure or something. That ought to do the trick."

"Thanks, I'll leave that to my local colleagues. But talking of doing the trick, I'm still puzzled. Where did the circus horses come in?"

"It's the same thing in a different setting. I was reminded of it when I saw circus animals being unloaded from a freighter at Hamilton quay.

"Children who go to the circus, and adults too, admire the way in which the circus horses step and prance in time to the music of the band. Not the Liberty horses, the special ones. It seems a wonderful training trick. But you know how it's done by now of course."

"I see, yes. It's actually the bandmaster who keeps time with the horses. Of course! Another childhood illusion shattered. Gillian, I do wish you'd teach me more. How about getting together when I return to London? The CID has need of you – and so do I!"

"I'd like that," Gillian murmured, "but you live at Woolwich, don't you? I hope you weren't thinking of going into the ferry game?"

Double Declutch

ROBIN BRAINE knew that he wasn't a popular chap. Acceptable, but not popular. True, he had a few friends at the garage where he worked but he would never be the centre of a gang of cronies, swapping jokes and going to football matches together.

He sighed. It had all started back in school, really. The moment Charlie Kipping realised the potential of Robin's first name and christened him Bird Brain the game was up. There were calls of "Watch the birdie!" in the playground and some of them went one better with Twitters, which could be abbreviated handily to Twit. What chance did he have?

He didn't allow it to get him down, though. Even when ringleader Charles moved in a few doors away in Hilltop Close he could afford to ignore the comings and goings and the cheerful late farewells which told of parties and continuing popularity.

After all, he and Charles had left school some years ago now; he had taken the local garage job and Charles departed every morning with a swish of tyres down the hill to be 'something in the City'. They exchanged few remarks these days and Robin firmly suppressed any lingering resentment – until, that is, Julia came on the scene.

Julia was not a local girl. She arrived, it was rumoured, from overseas where she had lived a life of affluent ease in the Kenyan uplands.

She was undeniably attractive. Her winsome freckled face and her preference for immaculate slacks and well-ironed bush shirts drew immediate attention. Heads turned, whispers flew and neighbours, mostly male, quickly called with offers of curtain-hanging, groceries, library information and transport around town.

Robin was one of the latter. His own car was not as large nor as impressive as the Kipping executive saloon but it was clean and bright and superbly maintained in every detail. Through the garage he had access to sophisticated equipment and every spare part he could ever want. That was one area in which he could more than compete with Charles, although he noted with some irritation that the luxury saloon was hastily polished and left obtrusively near Julia's gateway, rather than in its own garage.

Robin realised with a shock that he and Charles were becoming rivals of a sort; with a further shock he realised that it mattered. Julia, who had smiled at him and invited him to tea, began to fill his mind and his senses. She gave the impression that nobody was more welcome than he and that she could scarcely wait till their next meeting.

As the weeks went by Robin became infatuated. He could not bear to contemplate the possibility that Charles might be thinking the same thoughts and preening himself that he was the one enjoying Julia's favour. Robin took to imagining Julia in a more intimate setting, hanging on his arm, laughing and then suddenly serious, watching his lips drawing closer to hers.

He shook himself, however, as his morose nature, cultured by the dismal Bird Brain years, acknowledged that open-hearted Julia probably showed the same carefree aspect to everyone, including the self-confident Charles. If she did, Robin thought, he was lost.

He couldn't hope to match Charles' social ease and casual

lifestyle. Furthermore, he knew from former times that Charles would not allow himself to be sidelined lightly. He had a streak of cruel and ruthless ingenuity that had been directed not only at Robin but at several others. Charles would be a dangerous opponent.

Robin brooded over his problem. The more he did so the more desirable Julia became and the more likely it seemed that Charles would sweep her off her feet. He had money and all its trappings – expensive clothes and powerful car . . . Robin felt an unholy thrill of excitement. The car! That was the answer. Charles' car could be his salvation!

He ran over a scenario in his mind. Every weekday morning recently Charles came out to his car parked at the kerb, started the engine, pulled away and accelerated down the short hill. He didn't pause to try the brakes; he sailed off in his self-assured way, pushing in a Pet Shop Boys cassette and appearing at peace with the world.

Down at the bottom of the hill the Close came abruptly to a T-junction. A few yards away a solid stone wall awaited the driver who overshot the Stop sign. At one time the junction had been designated an Accident Black Spot; even with improved sight lines it was no place to lose control.

Robin's eyes narrowed in thought. If something were to happen to Charles' braking system, something that would affect both the hand and foot brakes, he would have no chance. The big car would rapidly get up to fifty or more and there would be no time to jam the lever into low ratio, even if it occurred to Charles to try it. His own car with its manual gears would be even more lethal but then Charles wouldn't be driving it. Yet there was a way!

The next day he put his plan into action. When Charles emerged from his front gate Robin was waiting for him. "Morning, Charles!" he said. "Don't see much of you these days. Keeping well?"

"Mustn't grumble," Charles replied without a smile. "What about you? Everything OK at the showroom?"

Robin seized his opportunity. "Not so bad," he said, "but speaking of cars I glanced in your side window and noticed you'd done 25,000 miles. Time for a service. Like me to do it for you? I can give you an unbeatable price!"

A look of interest came to Charles' face. "That's very civil of you, Bir – er – Robin," he said. "But do I really need a service? All the gadgets seem to be working properly."

Robin launched into an earnest discourse on dirt-clogged oil, wearing tyres, leaky gaskets and thinning brake pads. Charles listened closely, apparently impressed. "You mean the brakes could actually fail if they're not looked after?" he asked.

Robin redoubled his persuasive effort. He explained in detail how a sudden fault, or conceivably sabotage, could disable the finest car. Charles followed his words intently. He nodded frequently with understanding and finally told Robin to go ahead with the job right away.

"You're on!" Robin said. "You can borrow my car for today, if you like." Charles nodded again.

That evening Robin's task was done. He used all his knowledge and automotive skills to carry out the necessary work and returned the big car very carefully to its place at the side of the road. He noticed, in passing, that his own car had been returned.

Robin shut what he had done out of his mind. This wasn't murder or anything like that, he told himself. Charles might suffer fractured ribs, some concussion and maybe a few cuts, that was all. Enough to keep him temporarily out of circulation while he and Julia reached an understanding.

The next morning he went out onto the pavement to find, as

expected, an empty roadway. But although no car was to be seen he was shaken to find Charles lounging about, looking unconcerned. He hurried up to him, his mind in a spin.

"I say, where's your car?" he said, without preamble. "I left it here, last night, all finished."

Charles waved a hand vaguely. "Oh, didn't I tell you?" he said. "I've agreed to sell it to Julia, half-price. That's why I said 'yes' to the service. Julia needs a car. She's just this minute taken it for a test drive."

Robin stared at him in frozen horror. "No!" he shrieked. "You idiot! She can't . . ."

In desperation he whirled round, dashed to his garage, got out his own car and accelerated away frantically, passing Charles with a squeal of tyres.

As he did so he caught a glimpse of something out of the corner of his eye. Surely that was Julia by the gate, with Charles smirking over her shoulder? With sickening dread he stamped on the brake pedal and grabbed the little lever by the driving seat. Nothing happened.

The beautifully-maintained little car swooped towards the beckoning wall.

One Measle, One Mump

IT ALL STARTED over a round of drinks at the Scythe & Partridge. There was Charles, our resident pontificator, Percy the amateur psephologist and myself. (I once asked Percy what psephology was; he told me that it involved peering into the future – not to predict the result of the next election but to explain why the last one turned out as it did.)

Percy's friend, an American journalist called Gene, had joined us. The subject was the electoral scene. We had just been through a County Council election; the Conservatives had lost their overall majority but were still the largest single party at County Hall.

"You know your trouble?" said Gene. (We had found that most political discussions in the Scythe started off with some sure-fire diagnosis.) "You're going to be hung! Your whole trouble is going to be your plurality."

Percy and I looked at each other. "Speaking as a single man," said Percy virtuously, "I cannot . . ."

Gene waved him aside. "I mean your plurality at County Hall. You know what I mean – the situation where one political party has more seats than any other party but not more than all the others put together. In the States we have a word for that; we call it a plurality."

"And what do you call a majority?" I asked.

"Well, that would usually be an absolute majority. What I

believe you call an overall majority in this country. Isn't that right, Percy?"

"More or less," Percy murmured. "But strictly speaking the majority that you call a plurality should be a *plurity*. A plurality is really nothing more than the state of being plural like the number of beans that make five. That's English, rather than American."

"It's pedantry, rather than accuracy," Gene grumped.

They wrangled on amiably while I drank my bitter and contemplated the whole trouble of our plurality. "If you think about it," I observed to Charles, "there *is* something rather unwholesome about pluralness and the way it's taking over from singleness in general."

He cocked an eyebrow at me. "I mean," I plunged on, "we can leave to pundits like Gene and Percy the question of whether a county in a modern democracy can be administered under such conditions. I am thinking about plurality as a concept, and in particular how it is being debased through careless use of language."

Charles peered gravely at his tankard. "I suppose," he said cautiously, "that some people are guilty of using plurals where the singular would do. Why do they do it? Probably to gain effect, originally, but more usually these days as a habit of speech that has lost all its power through constant use. Mind you, the Quakers, who talk to thee (not you) individually, seem to be putting up some resistance."

"Yes, but we are all affected," I said, "even our Friends. Think back for a moment. When I mentioned administering a county under such conditions, did you twitch? I thought not. It should have been 'under such a condition' of course."

Charles opened his eyes more widely to indicate that he was turning his mind to the subject and I mused on. To someone interested in the quality of English language the trend to indiscriminate plurals was regrettable enough, I thought, but it was also insidious – so much so that it would not be enough to stamp on excess 'esses' like a gardener salting slugs. We ought to be attempting some kind of analysis of our troubles (whole or not) so that we could lead the way back to purer and more cogent English.

I settled back to think it out. In general, it seemed to me, words which struck one as singular, so to speak, (because they were so rarely seen) fell into two categories. There were those that were one of a pair and those that were one of a multitude. Maybe this pointed to the evolution of both literacy and numeracy from the primitive tribes whose only number-words were the equivalents of one, two and many.

What should be done about these categories, then? Admittedly, some ingenuity would be needed to cut a piece of paper with a scissor, or even a shear. But was it really impossible to conceive of a garment like an overall or a mechanism like a railway point? Must those words always march to Noah's tune, in twos?

I said as much to Charles. "Mm, as long as it doesn't go too far," he replied. "After all, the impact of the sinister coastal marauder would have been somewhat lessened under the title *Jaw*! It tends to stop you with one foot in the air, as you might be when putting on one tight or one trouser. In the same way, a joke that had you in a stitch would be no great shake."

"Maybe not," I acknowledged, "but in many instances (or many an instance!) the word we want to use does not need its twin standing alongside. Let us hunt the pair! Slice it apart and let each component stand on its own foot! Any self-respecting tick should be able to exist without a tock."

While Charles digested that I followed my line of thought.

Having dealt with doubles, what about crowds? Here, it appeared to me, the case was even more clear cut. Too often plurals were apt to be used merely to enlarge a statement and its effect for rhetorical purposes. When speaking of high fliers, for instance, it wasn't necessary to go beyond the upper reach of the atmosphere – or would that be an arm limitation?

By taking pain, it should be possible to come to a grip with the problem plural. A stuck-up Soubrette needed no replication; giving herself an air and a grace should be sufficient. We could then observe the result through our rented opus glass.

With an effort, I considered, we could probably purge our writing. But the misfortune was that the tide of plurality was sweeping over ordinary colloquial speech as well. The general exaggeration was becoming self-defeating. As Gilbert once remarked: "When everyone is somebodee, then no one's anybody!"

In fact, I realised, one can scarcely say anything these days (this day?) without the aid of the ubiquitous plural. Who would be ready to admit that he had suffered from a measle, far less gone to the dog? It would be vaguely demeaning to invite a friend to one's dig, while to talk of throwing a die would seem to imply in some way that you couldn't afford two of them.

From the time we learned about the bird and the bee we had been immersed in multiple words and multiple images – and therefore, surely, imprecise and unfocussed thought. We travelled by British Rail but not by British Airway. We could visit Thame but not Devize. We played cricket but not rounder.

"Away with this monstrous regiment of plurals!" I exclaimed, coming out of my reverie. "No esses except on a Grand Prix race track!"

Gene and Percy stared at me open-mouthed and even Charles blinked. "You what?" ventured Percy.

"Plurality, that's our whole trouble!" I said. "Gene's right. But we're all affected, not just the County Council. Some of us even have the acute form – double plurality. On the village green the batsmen have their elevenses before continuing their inningses. There's even a quadruple form in the nursery – 'lots and lots'!"

I looked round. A hush seemed to have fallen over the nearby tables and glances were being exchanged. I turned back and picked up my glass nonchalantly. The others did the same.

"Gentlemen!" said Charles quietly, "the Anti-Plurality League is now in session. Slogan: No Doubles! in the bar or on the tennis court. End of opening remark. I give you a thank for your attention. Cheer!"

Somebody Else

THE noises started early in the morning chill. Hardly had the street lamps winked out, one by one, when the first vans arrived.

Melissa listened to the 'clomp' of drivers' doors punctuating the baritone squeak of hinges as the rear doors were opened. Men dragged out bars of metal which scraped and rang against the cobbles.

Rods and links were fitted together with a thin melodic tinkle, accompanied by grunts of effort and the occasional low remark. It reminded Melissa of an orchestra tuning up, with the weaving hum of strings and woodwind being decorated by tapping from the percussion and the brief shrieks of the flutes. There was the same air of expectancy.

Canvas bundles shook, unfolded themselves and stretched, like hounds waking from sleep. They took shape along either side of the street, all sizes and colours, in an ordered row like a motley army falling in on parade. Crates and boxes were unloaded and the vans moved away. The market stalls were ready for business.

Melissa had once had a paper round which included the street market. She had risen at dawn to collect the newspapers, already sorted by Mr Ibrahim, from the shop on the corner. Often, as she strode through the empty streets, she had imagined herself as an intrepid journalist tracking down a source intent on her scoop, notebook and camera at the ready.

Somebody Else

Instead she was up early once again researching an article on street activities for the local tourist board. Her careful prose was likely to be sub-edited and 'angled' for the tourist literature – 'mangled' was a truer description, she thought.

It was a long way from intrepid journalism; she might as well be somebody else entirely. In a way she was, since she wrote under the pen-name of Tour-guide Tim – not that the tourist would care, of course.

As a youngster she had taken extra copies of the tabloids in her canvas satchel once a week so that the street traders could scan the headlines over their first mug of tea. Many of them were market families who had occupied the same pitches for years. They were always grateful for the papers.

It was one way in which Mr Ibrahim looked after the interests of his customers. "That is how to do business," he informed Melissa seriously. "That is how you make friends. That is how you live your life. Truly. You are living your life among your friends, not your enemies."

Melissa couldn't imagine Mr Ibrahim having enemies. When he was sorting his papers, counting the stationery packets or arranging pyramids of chocolate bars he wore a sports shirt and cardigan and hummed to himself. When he opened the shop, though, he changed into a smart grey tunic and spoke with solemn care. He delivered pleasant little homilies to Melissa, tilting his head from side to side like a bird listening for a worm.

"People are the same everywhere, isn't it? Always the same. They do not learn to recognise themselves, so they are not content." He gave Melissa a meaning look.

"They look in the mirror every morning and what do they see? They do not see themselves – they see someone else. Truly! You know whom they see?" He leaned forward earnestly. "They see the person they *want* to be. Not who they are, mind you, who they want to be. Wonderful, it is. Everybody wants to be somebody else."

Mr Ibrahim nodded wisely. "You know the man who is being awkward and bashful – can't say boo to the goose? He is sitting in front of the telly and thinking he can be a success like Bob Monkhouse or Bruce Forsyth. Easy!

"Or the girl who cannot make a seam on a handkerchief? What is she thinking? Not long before she is presenting her spring collection in Paris!" Melissa grinned at a recent memory.

"The other way, also. There is Professor Bascombe from number twenty-seven; always pays his paper bill regularly. Do you know, he is an authority on nuclear physics at Loughborough? But modest he is – oh, nothing compared with that Stephen Hawking at Cambridge. Lucky to have a chair at all, he is thinking. He told me!" Mr Ibrahim turned back to the till, point made.

His words came back to Melissa as she followed the postman on his round through the market. She watched his quick fluent walk. Did people write letters to stallholders, she wondered. And would the postie deliver them?

She paused at one stall and looked at its serried shelves of boxes. There were irons and frying pans, shampoos and sponges, vases and table lamps in a steep cardboard cliff. Umbrellas hung from the roof and fat electric fans stood on the floor. Sheets and bath towels cascaded over the piles of merchandise.

A man who was evidently the stallholder stood proprietorially near a low rostrum, fingertips outspread on a folding table. He cut an impressive figure. His steady eyes and thoughtful expression inspired confidence, while his neatly waved hair showed that he took trouble with his appearance.

His clothes conveyed the same message. A cutaway coat with its carnation buttonhole revealed a frogged waistcoat and rose-coloured shirt. His cuffs were discreet and his shoes polished. it was as if he were ready for a spotlight to illuminate him.

"Good morning, miss," he said pleasantly. "Up with the lark? That's the way. Snap up the bargains while they're there, eh?"

Melissa smiled. "Maybe. Depends what you're offering. Are you really going to sell all these different things today?"

The man smiled in his turn. "Would that surprise you, young lady? You can't imagine the contents of a small shop being disposed of in a few hours, is that it? Don't worry. It's all a question of technique – a matter of know-how. A master salesman doesn't have to know his stock; he has to know his customers."

"I'm sure you're right," said Melissa. "But still . . ."

"Nothing to it," he went on. "You want to know how it's done? Listen! You start with the earwig."

"The what?" Melissa said, startled.

"The earwig. 'Ere we go, get it?" He flung out a hand. "Come on girls, look no further, here you are, every one guaranteed, been here thirty years – that sort of thing. Then comes the costume."

"The costume?" gasped Melissa.

"Yes, the costume. Cost you much more in the shops, see? Twice the price at Asda. Have you seen what they're asking in Tesco's? Make them think it's a bargain, that's the idea. After that you get to the mortar."

Melissa looked at him. "You're making this up!" she said.

"Not at all. The mortar. More to come! That's when you slap on an extra tube of toothpaste – or a shoe-brush. For nothing. All in the price, see? It's irresistible. And then at last you give them the never-mind."

Melissa couldn't suppress a gurgle of laughter. "Of course! Mustn't forget that!" she nodded.

"Certainly not. The never-mind always works. Never mind

ten pound, never mind six pound or four fifty." He smacked his hand down. "Three quid, who wants it? You at the back, madam. And you sir. That's right, hurry up, they won't last all day!"

He paused and stretched has arms wide. "Selling isn't just a job. It's a study of human nature, a view of living, an art form. Yes, it's painting a picture with words."

"A picture of an earwig in costume with mortar?" suggested Melissa.

"Sure, why not? It's . . ."

He was interrupted by a short, tubby man with a ginger moustache. He bustled in wiping his hands on a dirty apron and leapt onto the rostrum.

"Right, let's get on with it," he said. "Same as usual; I'll knock the stuff out, Harry. You be ready with the boxes." He raised his voice. "Now then, girls, look no further, here you are . . ."

Melissa turned away, avoiding Harry's eye. Mr Ibrahim was right. Everyone did want to be somebody else.

One Step Ahead

THE roll of banknotes in Susan's hand was in one way insignificant. Both its size and weight were negligible but as she looked round the living room in Graham's flat the money became curiously heavy with responsibility.

"Hide this," Graham had instructed her, "so that I can't find it, even in my own home. If you can do that you'll be cunning enough for our partnership."

For the umpteenth time Susan wondered how she had got into this situation. Desperately she considered and rejected various hiding places while a tinkle of cups and spoons came from the adjoining kitchenette. The walls, the sofa and the bookcase stared back at her unhelpfully. She tried to shake off a shivery feeling of conspiracy as she made her choice.

A few minutes later Graham re-entered with a tray of tea and biscuits. He put it down on the card table and rubbed his hands together. "Well concealed, is it?" he grinned. "Well now, let's see!"

He quested round the room like a caged ferret. Drawers were opened and shut, pictures were turned and ornaments probed. Every book on the shelves had to be pulled out and examined; he even groped behind the radiator. Susan stood, cup and saucer in hand, watching him.

Graham finally poured himself a cup and slumped onto the sofa. "OK, I give up," he admitted. "Where's the wonga?"

Susan quietly put her cup back on the tray and shifted it to an empty chair. She lifted the green baize cloth from the table top and revealed the flat wad of notes. "I thought you might not think of moving the tray once you'd put it down," she said demurely. "Have another cup."

Graham put the palms of his hands together and inclined his head. "Well done, princess!" he said. "Thou art indeed ready for our enterprise. I go now to purchase the requisites. But," – he dropped the theatrical tone as he left the room – "watch out for Simon. I wouldn't put it past him to nick the lolly when you're not looking."

Simon was Graham's lodger. Apparently he was out of work and lived permanently in a torn T-shirt and jeans. From the start his manner had seemed rather shifty to Susan but she didn't like to comment on a friend of Graham's. However when things started disappearing from the flat Graham suspected Simon had a drug problem and gave him notice. He was to leave at the end of the week.

Susan rearranged the baize cloth, tidied up the tray and paused for some time to gaze out of the window at the bare trees in the little square below and Graham's retreating footprints in the snow beneath them. She cast her mind back over recent events.

It had all started one winter's day when Graham suggested that they go to Aviemore. Susan couldn't ski and was more than a little wobbly on a pair of skates but Graham didn't have winter sports in mind. Nor romance, unfortunately. He wanted to play bridge.

When they had first met, at last year's office Christmas party, Susan quickly learned that he was good-humoured, quick-witted and unattached. He also had a passion for playing cards. Well, it made a change from football or darts, Susan thought, but it wasn't likely to form a bond between them.

But there she was wrong. Graham, it turned out, was addicted to contract bridge – and the serious variety, at that. Before she could prevent him he was extolling the virtues of the duplicate game, where the luck of the deal was eliminated. He expanded on the psychology of the auction and the science of dummy play. There was no stopping him.

Susan had enjoyed rummy as a youngster and taken a liking to whist, later on. However when he urged her to try competitive bridge she was reluctant.

"Bridge players are all sharp-eyed professional women or elderly colonels, aren't they?" she said doubtfully. "And every game seems to end in some sort of squabble. It doesn't appeal to me much."

Graham's keenness was unquenchable. "You're thinking of West End clubs and places like that," he said, "where they play rubber bridge for money. I'm talking about the real game, tournament bridge, where the players are loyal partners and what you win are cups and master points, not cash."

"Master points? That sounds awfully high-powered," she said tentatively. "I'm not brainy enough, I'm afraid."

"Nonsense!" said Graham breezily. "If you can play whist you can play bridge. There's only the bidding to learn. I'll teach you!"

He did teach her, with geniality and patience. In fact, to her regret, he seemed to be more interested in the tuition than in her.

She rapidly discovered that there was not only the bidding to learn, as he claimed. There were many other things – conventions, proprieties, squeezes and sacrifices, to say nothing of tactics and guile.

It was the last of these that was the trouble. Graham wanted them to form a partnership and got to the Aviemore Congress, to compete against scores of other pairs and maybe win a prize or two. And some coveted green master points. He assembled the money for train fares, entrance fees and other expenses but last-minute doubts crept in.

"There's just one thing," he told her. "You're a good enough player by now; good enough to win a junior competition with me, anyway. But you're still too – too *honest*! Your bids and plays are an open book. No guile.

"You've got to learn to think deviously – to keep one step ahead all the time. That's the way to win." And that was what had led to the little test of subtlety – the hiding of the money. Susan was glad she had passed the test and hoped it would help to awaken Graham's interest in her as a person rather than a bridge player.

As she turned with the tray in her hands the bedroom door moved a few inches and Simon stood there, blinking slyly. He looked at her with a knowing smile and Susan realised that he must have been there for some time. He came forward with his usual furtive air.

"Hallo, Susan," he began. "I thought I heard you. Where's Graham? Gone out, has he? Pity. I was going to ask him to lend me a few quid. I'm a bit short at the moment; you know how it is. I say, you couldn't let me have a spot of cash, could you? Just till Friday?"

Susan backed away. "Sorry, Simon, I can't help," she said. "There's nothing – I mean, I've got nothing on me at the moment. Sorry."

Simon's smile widened into a wolfish grin. "Nothing, eh? Nothing at all? Well, well! I'll have to see what I can find for myself, shan't I?" As he moved towards the card table Susan saw with a sudden flood of relief that Graham had returned and was opening the front door into the tiny hall.

Simon had his back to Graham. He leered at Susan as he

turned up the corner of the baize cloth. "I wonder what's under here," he murmured. "A little something to tide me over, perhaps?"

He drew the cloth back complacently, exposing the blank table top. She saw his expression change to a scowl. "Where is it?" he snarled. "I know it's here. What have you done with it, you bitch?" He turned viciously but before he could make a further move Graham was in the room, grim and menacing.

"That's enough, Simon!" he said. "That's the end. Get out before I throw you out. Go on, get out! Now!"

Simon hesitated a moment. He looked from one of them to the other, weighing his chances. Then, with a look of hatred, he slunk out across the hall and through the open door.

Graham removed the tray from Susan's hands and put it down. He took her in his arms and held her. "Sorry about that," he said. "Good thing I came back when I did. He didn't touch you, did he? Are you all right?"

Susan nestled slightly against him. "Quite all right," she assured him.

"And he didn't get the money, either? Nice one, Sue! Where was it, by the way?"

Susan turned, casually opened the pack of cards lying on the table and shook out the banknotes. "As you told me to, I managed to keep one step ahead," she said.

Command Decision

Admiral of the Fleet James Granville sat with his chin resting on his folded hands. He was alone. His blue eyes, roaming widely in deep thought, surveyed the scene before him.

At his feet the torrent, swollen by recent rains, rushed past. The swirls and eddies in the swift turbulence toyed with small pieces of flotsam, impelling them this way and that as if they were weightless.

The open ground on the near bank was sodden and well trampled. He could see the grass beaded with droplets in the weak sunlight, the interweaving trails of many footprints and the sharp line of stone casting its shadow at the water's edge.

On the far side lay a glistening expanse of grey, dappled with sunlight and marked with fissures and irregularities. It stretched away, like the flank of a bathing elephant, to a distant ribbon of brown and green, earth and foliage alternating in a pattern of early summer.

The admiral turned his gaze downstream. The churning water ran almost straight for a long way from his position and then, with a careless swirl, disappeared round a bend. Martha's Corner, they called it.

James Granville had never travelled beyond Martha's Corner – it was considered too hazardous for him to do so – but he knew what lay beyond. At least, he had received reports.

Command Decision

It was said, by Robert and others, that somewhere beyond the corner the roiling current ran more swiftly still until it suddenly dived into the earth, leaving only a small backwater of slowly rotating debris. Nothing that had entered that infernal mouth had ever been known to return.

The guardian backwater lay within the sphere of influence of the other side. It was a place of foam and turmoil, so it was said; a place to daunt the spirit. And it was there that the prize was to be grasped – there that the most intrepid craft would gain the reward.

The admiral was presented with a problem – possibly the most complex problem of his life. It was vital that one of the boats under his command, presently drydocked, should attain the hidden backwater. Only in that way could the watercourse be flanked. Rival flotillas must be given an unmistakable warning; only thus could naval supremacy be re-established.

The dilemma lay in the choice of craft and the timing of her launch. Should he entrust the mission to *Lucifer*, with her speed and her ability to ride high in the water but her matchboard-thin hull? Or should he prefer *Captain's Log*, sturdy and able to withstand the forces of wind and water but ponderous and slow to manoeuvre?

The admiral tilted his head slightly, lips compressed. Should the choice fall instead on little *Sardinia*? She was of more modern construction, with her coamings of metal plate, but she was as yet unproven and even considered by some to be unlucky.

Then there was the question of the launch itself. If it took place too early the chosen boat would find herself at the mercy of cross-currents and rip tides in those uncharted reaches. She would list and shimmy in her death-dance, finally broaching-to and being overwhelmed.

On the other hand if the launching operation were delayed

too long the falling waters would leave unknown shoals and obstructions to imperil the bold vessel. Her progress would be steady and triumphant until suddenly a lurch, a jar and a sickening halt at a crazy angle would signal failure.

The exact moment had to be seized, with flair and vision. All the considerations must be factored in, allowing proportionate weight to both pragmatism and naval superstition. The enterprise required inspiration and imagination, as well, for its ultimate success.

The admiral pondered. The loneliness of power was not a background spectre. He faced a command decision but it was a decision he did not fear to take, since on his shoulders the responsibilities of command no longer sat drear and awesome. However he was not quite ready to commit himself to precipitate action in this present venture.

He looked up as Robert came into view, presumably waiting for his orders. The admiral frowned slightly as he surveyed his resources. Robert was affable, dependable even, but being a little older than himself was cautious and inclined to raise questions when given a commission.

James Granville's eyes narrowed. The failure of this sortie was not to be contemplated.

Only the previous week a foraging party of his had returned empty-handed from the field. Before that various construction projects had not achieved their potential or even been left unfinished. There was marked room for improvement. This time, success was vital.

The admiral's chin lifted. He came to his command decision, smoothly and with certainty. *Lucifer* should undertake the daring venture. His spirit would keep her company and his reputation would hang upon her fragile frame.

He turned to Robert. His instructions were clear and concise.

Command Decision

Lucifer was to be made ready and an observer was to be posted near Martha's Corner.

He listened to Robert's queries and reservations wearily. Robert was unused to the pressures of command. His forte lay in following orders, if with reluctance, not in formulating them. Furthermore he was unable to place himself in the shoes of others, as an imaginative commander must.

He forgot, or perhaps ignored, the fact that James Granville, while in control locally, was not a free agent. He too had a higher command – a supreme authority whose directives could not be disobeyed. Since Robert was part of the same organisation he should have understood but he gave no sign of it.

The admiral straightened his shoulders, brushing aside Robert's doubts and plaints. The decision had been taken and the time for action had arrived. As Robert departed for his post James Granville rose to his feet with resolute mien. He stepped back to his personal sea-locker and scanned the contents.

Putting aside the solid wooden *Captain's Log* and the river-worthy sardine tin he lifted out *Lucifer*, his pride and joy. Quickly he fitted a matchstick mast equipped with a fold of newspaper for a sail. He was on the very point of launching the matchbox into the gutter stream when a voice from behind him cut into his thoughts.

"Jimmy? Come along – dinner time. And don't forget to wash your hands first."

Resignedly he called to Robert and they made their way up the garden path. A supreme command decision had been taken!

Passing the Test

THE advertisement in the newspaper was crisp and to the point: *VACANCY for physiologist on expedition to Matto Grosso. Briefing for applicants: Lecture Room B, Masson Memorial Hall, 7 p.m., Tuesday 24th February.*

Charlotte put the paper down on the breakfast table and gazed thoughtfully at the icicles outside the casement window. The euphoria of successfully completing her studies at the far-off medical college was wearing off. Yesterday, a short break from white coats and the smell of ether had seemed attractive; she could enjoy some sort of social life while writing off for a postgraduate position at a teaching hospital.

But life was suddenly and curiously flat after the bustling tempo of college life, with its unexpected concepts and fresh material every day. She realised that she was missing the challenge of the new; here, perhaps, was an opportunity to use her new knowledge. If she didn't take it she would go on to specialist training and then perhaps into general practice, in which any further stimulus would be unlikely.

The thought of being a cog in the NHS machine was not appealing. Charlotte glanced again at the advertisement. She seemed to remember that the Matto Grosso was a vast massif of jungle swamps somewhere in the interior of Brazil. The climate would be very different from the bracing cold of an English February, with its chill carpet of snow.

Passing the Test

On an impulse she decided to attend the advertised briefing. After all, it would commit her to nothing. She might even find out more about medical-type appointments to overseas projects, to say nothing of naval opportunities.

Arriving at the Memorial Hall on Tuesday evening she was directed to a lecture room furnished with the usual drab assortment of steel-framed tables and chairs. At one end a dais bore a larger cloth-covered table, a lectern and two whiteboards with coloured pens. For a moment she had the impression of being back in medical school, weary with homework and burdened with exercise books and course notes.

However the differences soon became apparent. No light-hearted hubbub arose from those who had arrived before her. Nor was there much similarity in age and appearance. Looking around her she saw a surprising variety of faces and ages, men and women of all types in all kinds of clothes.

In one corner she recognised a doctor from the local clinic. She recalled that his name was Fonseca; he wasn't wearing a white coat but a whiff of ether drifted into her imagination.

Charlotte moved to a table in the second row and sat down at it. A moment later the other seat at the table was taken by a young man in jeans and pullover. He smiled at her briefly and then sprawled back in his chair with an easy grace. She noticed that his eyes were hazel and his hair fell into rebellious twirls of golden brown. He looked about him with casual candour.

As the clock over the dais clicked to one minute past seven a tall man in well-cut tweeds strode into the room, swinging the door shut decisively behind him. He sprang energetically onto the dais, ignoring the set of steps to one side, dropped a clipboard with a sheaf of papers onto the table and turned to face his audience.

"Good evening, good evening!" he said heartily. "Glad to see so many of you here. Shows that the spirit of adventure isn't dead, what?" He projected a satisfied look over the assembly and Charlotte noticed his even teeth and tanned complexion. His grey eyes, under bushy eyebrows, seemed to quarter the room like game dogs, missing nothing.

"Righto, let's make a start. My name's Thorby, Geoff Thorby, and I'm helping Lord Cawston put together an expedition to South America to collect and preserve endangered botanical species. The party will include an ecologist, a taxonomist and a phytogeographer among others. They will be looking at the bryology and pteridology of the region and will take a particular interest in the epiphytes."

His smile widened. "Are you with me so far?" There was a general shaking of heads and some of those seated at the tables looked at each other blankly, as though wondering if they were in the right meeting. Charlotte exchanged a look with her table companion and received a wink and an engaging grin.

"Not to worry!" Thorby said heartily. "These people have already been chosen as botanical specialists. They are the core of the expedition, if you like. But in addition to them we also have porters and Indian guides plus a wireless operator and a logistics officer. His job is to keep us fed and watered.

"Now, we need one last person – a physiologist. His or her responsibility will be to monitor the health of the whole party, to prevent infection by hygienic and medicinal means and to cope with any injuries. The physiologist will also be required to measure the fitness of the European members and to write a report on our return to the UK.

"So clearly a certain kind of person is needed. We are looking for someone with medical competence, someone with fitness and stamina, if possible with a knowledge of Portuguese and some experience of living and travelling in the open. We shall be away for at least five months so there must be no home ties."

Passing the Test

"We shall of course expect the successful applicant to be enthusiastic about the project – to have a sense of enterprise and adventure. One more thing. The person chosen will need to demonstrate that he or she can act independently if necessary, can remain calm in the face of hazard and is capable of reasoning through problems and difficulties."

Thorby turned and picked up the sheaf of papers. "First of all, then, I want you to fill in these application forms and return them to me before you leave. More particularly, though, we want to assess your suitability as well as your qualifications. To do this we have set up an initiative test this weekend near the village of Braythorpe, about fifteen miles away. I expect you know it.

"Here's the drill. Your applications will be studied tomorrow and if you are to be invited to the initiative test you will receive a telephone call within the next day or so. Please keep Saturday clear for the moment."

Thorby pointed to a man in a raincoat at the front. "Now, sir, if you'll kindly help me by handing out these forms I can deal with any queries. Thank you." He straightened up. "Right. I expect you'll want to know a lot more. Questions, anyone?"

Charlotte was reminded of a hearty character bounding through French windows and asking if anyone was for tennis. A man in the front row raised a diffident hand, perhaps fearing that if he acted like a schoolboy he would fail Thorby's initiative test on the spot.

"Erm – you mentioned hazard," he said hesitantly. "Exactly what are the – the risks associated with this venture?"

"Oh, just the usual ones!" Thorby replied breezily. "Malaria, dengue fever, snake bite, curare poisoning from Indian arrows – that sort of thing. Then there's drowning in a swamp – or being eaten by alligators and piranha if you're careless. Routine stuff. Of course you'll be required to sign an indemnity paper before we leave." He laughed. "We don't want any lawsuits later, do we?"

He looked round. "Any other points?"

A woman with combed-back hair and a grim expression spoke from the next table. "So what's in it for us?" she asked. "What kind of pay do we get for this job?"

Thorby bent a look on her. "In the field everything will be 'found' for you," he said in a dead tone. "Food, equipment, weapons and supplies. Money will not be needed; there'll be nowhere to spend it. A small – repeat, *small* – honorarium will be offered at the end of the expedition. Your main reward will be the experience. All right?"

She did not respond. Charlotte saw that several people had declined the application forms and were leaving. She suspected that Thorby had made the prospects deliberately uninviting to weed out those who were less keen. A group of six or seven remained and were filling in the forms; she decided to take Thorby on at his own game and go after the vacancy.

The young man next to her seemed to have taken the same decision. He looked up from his form and raised an eyebrow at her. "Well, are you going to have a go?" he said.

"Why not?" she replied. "I've always wanted to see Rio de Janeiro."

"Too late for the Mardi Gras parade this year," he commented, "but a stroll though the tropical jungle should be nearly as exciting, I should think."

It turned out that his name was James Ballater and he was, like her, in the process of finishing his medical training. His long flexible fingers circled the application form as he filled it in; maybe, she thought, he was destined for a career in the operating theatre.

She went up to the dais to hand in her completed form. As

Thorby took it from her their eyes met for a moment. She detected a glint of amusement in his expression too and resolved that, come what may, she would not be bluffed by his presentation. Emerging into the cold night air she felt somewhat amused herself. She had spotted, and quietly frustrated, James Ballater's attempt to read the telephone number on her form.

By Thursday lunchtime the meeting in the lecture room had more or less faded from her mind as she leafed through correspondence from bursars and registrars. The country was supposed to be short of doctors but she didn't detect any great rush for her services. She moped. When the telephone rang she was not immediately prepared for Thorby's brisk voice.

"Miss Tamlyn? This is Geoff Thorby. About the botanical expedition. Your application has been found satisfactory and I am therefore inviting you to attend our initiative test. Can you get yourself to the Three Acorns at Braythorpe by fifteen hundred hours on Saturday? You can? Good! No need to bring anything with you apart from a warm jacket and stout shoes. I look forward to seeing you, then. Goodbye!"

Mr Thorby was undoubtedly economical with words, she reflected. Maybe he would welcome the same trait in others. She supposed that there would be no place for chatterers on a jungle expedition.

The mention of the jacket and shoes seemed to indicate that the test would be out of doors. She hoped that Thorby wasn't going to lead a makeshift expedition across frozen fields and through icy hedgerows. She didn't think she could start a fire for a brew-up by rubbing two sticks together, or whatever the survival technique was.

That Saturday afternoon she wrapped herself in an old lambswool coat, drove out to the village of Braythorpe and parked behind the pub that Thorby had mentioned. She found a knot of people gathered in the forecourt, beating their mittened hands together and breathing plumes of vapour into the still air. James, now in a chunky Fair Isle sweater, emerged from the group and greeted her.

"Hi! I'm so glad you've been invited," he said. "Looks like being good clean fun, don't you think?"

Charlotte was about to express a few doubts when Thorby emerged from the saloon door and marched purposefully across the yard. A whistle swung from a lanyard round his neck.

"Right you are, chaps!" he called out. "This way, if you please. It's just a short walk to the test site."

Charlotte didn't mind being one of the 'chaps' if that was what Thorby wanted. James was asking her to call him Jim and was ushering her courteously before him. Probably, she thought, on a jungle trail any sexual niceties would vanish after the first bend.

The party followed Thorby along the road for half a mile, picking their way through the slush, and then turned into a lane. Passing a copse shrouded in white they entered a gate in the next field and came to a halt.

In front of them the snowy field rose in a gentle slope. Near the far side a small hut stood forlorn. A single line of footprints led to it from where they were standing. To one side of them was a weathered barn; a dingy sign over the door proclaimed Braythorpe Sports Club.

Charlotte could see a set of tyre tracks leading from the barn to the hut and then away to a gate into the next field. Behind the gate a grey Land Rover could be seen; evidently it had made the tracks. Apart from the footprints and the tracks the snow was undisturbed.

At the corner of the barn five men were waiting for them. They were in casual battledress with scarves and gloves and all of them managed to look uneasy. They shifted from foot to foot in the snow and muttered in low tones. Round the neck of each one was a cardboard placard with a letter on it.

Thorby gathered his party together with a round gesture. "All right, chaps, your initiative test starts now. Up there in that hut a murder has been committed. You are the detective assigned to the case. From certain other evidence you know that the murderer is one of the five suspects you see here. They are labelled A to E, as you see."

The military volunteers looked even more embarrassed. They smiled and chuckled; one or two nudged their companions with their elbows gleefully.

Thorby ignored the byplay. "The footprints you see leading to the hut are those of the victim. His body was discovered a short time ago by a farmer in his Land Rover, whose tracks you can also see. He was met at that gate by his foreman, who informed the police by telephone, but neither they nor the doctor have yet arrived. You are on the scene and have the opportunity to investigate.

"You may look around for any clues. If you go into the hut you will see a bale of straw wrapped in a sack with a turnip attached to one end; that represents the body.

"You may put one question to each of the suspects over there. The rules are the same as in the well-known party game. They will all tell the truth except the assassin, who is allowed to lie. Understood? I shall play the role of the farmer and you can ask me a question too if you wish. You can also confer among yourselves if you want to.

"After forty-five minutes I shall ask you individually – not as a group – to tell me the name, or rather the letter, of the suspect whom you intend to charge with the murder and, of course, the reason why you have decided on that suspect. Off you go, then. Good luck!"

Charlotte gulped with dismay as Thorby strolled off to chat to the five suspects. How on earth was she to determine which of the five was the guilty party? There seemed to be nothing whatsoever to go on.

She frowned in concentration. What was it Thorby had said on Tuesday? It was something about an ability to remain calm and to reason through a problem. That was evidently what he was looking for here. She closed her eyes and tried to summon up calmness and reason.

She opened them again as James came to her side and bent a quizzical look on her. "How about that?" he remarked. "What he wants is a detective, not an explorer. I haven't the slightest idea what to do, have you?"

"Not much," Charlotte confessed. "But if we look around something should occur to us. I believe that what is wanted is what they call lateral thinking."

"Lateral thinking?" he said, wide-eyed. "Well, that lets me out. I have enough trouble trying to think forward and remember backward, in the normal way. How does one think laterally?"

Charlotte gave him a sideways look. She chuckled as the thought struck her that it might be taken as a lateral look. Quickly she shook her head and composed herself.

"One begins by taking the problem seriously," she suggested. "First of all, the problem must be soluble or there wouldn't be any point in setting it. That makes it easier than a real-life problem which may not have a solution. Yes?

"Second, there must be a method of differentiating between the volunteer suspects. They all look much alike, apart from the placards, so the differentiation will no doubt be found through questioning. However we must work out what question to ask."

"I say, you're a whizz at this stuff!" James said. "Your name isn't Miss Marple, is it?"

"Do you mind?" Charlotte laughed. "I'm not quite in my seventies yet! Now the third point. There must be something significant about the field and its contents, otherwise the exercise could have been mounted just as well back in the lecture room, couldn't it?

"So, the thing to do is look around, as Thorby said, and that will suggest a question or two to ask. Why don't you go and have a look at the Land Rover – and the hut if you can reach it? I'll examine the tracks and take a look in the barn. Then we can compare notes, OK?"

James nodded and departed. She looked round to find the start of the line of footprints. As she moved forward she overheard some conversation from the rest of the group.

"I suspect Thorby's being devious," said an insistent high-pitched voice. "The natural action is to take a look inside the hut. But we can't do that without trampling over the footprints and the vehicle tracks. Maybe that's the nub of the problem. Any ideas, anyone?"

Charlotte chuckled to herself once again. She wondered how Jim would tackle the situation. It was admittedly a good notion to examine the marks in the snow before any of the others walked over them on their way to the hut. She crossed over the footprints and bent over them.

At first glance the prints seemed normal, with soles and heels outlined and slight scuff marks from one print to the next, as would be expected in deep snow. The heel marks were deeper than the soles and seemed to be round rather than semi-circular but otherwise they were unremarkable. She wondered what sort of shoes or boots had made them.

She raised her eyes to the hut again and a thought struck her. There was only one line of footprints, naturally, because the unfortunate victim had walked to the hut but not away from it.

There was also just one set of Land Rover tracks, made by the farmer driving towards and away from the hut. So where were the tracks of the murderer? He could hardly have dropped in by helicopter to do the deed.

Was the farmer the murderer, then? It would be no use asking Thorby, acting as the farmer. Being allowed to lie he would obviously deny any wrongdoing. Could this be a case of suicide? But no – Thorby had stated at the beginning that one of the suspects by the barn was the guilty party.

Feeling that she was making no progress she wandered over to the barn and peered inside. In the gloom she could make out some rusty farm machinery in the shadows. Closer to the door was a pile of sporting accessories including tennis racquets, baseball gloves, croquet mallets and golf clubs. There was also athletics equipment; she could see a punch-ball and a rowing machine. A vaulting pole, a javelin and a pair of stilts leaned against the wall among an assortment of weights and Indian clubs.

She peered closely at every item for some time and a glimmer of an idea came to her. As she left the barn she bumped into James returning from his foray.

"Hallo!" he said breathlessly. "What have you found? I haven't had any luck, I'm afraid. There's nothing odd about the Land Rover by the gate. The tyres match the tracks. I managed to reach the hut from the rear, without disturbing the marks in the snow, but there's nothing helpful in there either. Just the sack and the turnip, as Thorby said."

Charlotte drew him to one side. "Never mind," she said, "I think I've got an idea. See what you think of it. Now, what is the most baffling thing about this test, would you say?"

James narrowed his eyes in thought. "I suppose it's that set of footprints," he mused, "I mean that there's only one line of them.

Passing the Test

The murderer had to reach the hut somehow. Even if he was already there when his victim arrived he would still have to get away afterwards. We know that the snow had fallen by then because of the victim's footprints. So how did the criminal make his escape?"

"There is a possible way," Charlotte told him. "He could have used the murdered man's tracks!"

"That wouldn't work, I'm afraid," James said. "If he walked backwards in the victim's footmarks then his own would be impressed on top of them. But Thorby told us that the footprints are those of the victim, and he's not allowed to lie – unless of course he's the murderer."

"It could work – there is a way!" Charlotte said earnestly. "Listen, I found a pair of stilts among other bits and pieces in the barn. I felt their tips and they were wet and cold. Also, if you examine the footprints themselves you will see that the heel-marks are round and very deep. I bet the murderer got away from the hut by using the stilts and walking in the existing heel marks. What do you think?"

Surprise and delight lit up James' face. "That's bloody fantastic!" he said. "Sorry, pardon my French. I mean that's highly ingenious! I should never have thought of that. But I wonder why the murderer left the stilts behind. I should have taken them with me if I were he.

"Good point, Jim," said Charlotte. "Probably they had to be left in the barn in order for us to have a chance to draw the correct inference. But we haven't finished. We still don't know which of the suspects is the guilty party. How do we identify him?"

"We'll have to ask them, I guess," James offered.

"Yes, but what do we ask them? It's no good asking if they used the stilts. They will all say no, four of them truthfully and one falsely. That'll get us nowhere."

"Ah! It's my turn to have an idea!" James gripped her hands looking immensely excited. "Remember those children's puzzles which involve members of weird tribes, some of whom always tell the truth and others always lie? Usually the tricky answer is to link them together through the question you put to them.

"In this case we ask every suspect: 'Did you see the man next to you walking on stilts across the field?' One of them will give the correct answer: 'yes'."

"And one of them will give a false answer!" Charlotte chuckled. "He'll have to, because if he tells the truth the single 'yes' from the other man will incriminate him. So how does that help?"

"Well, it would narrow it down to just two of them," James remarked, suddenly glum. "I've done my bit; now it's your turn."

Charlotte's face lit up in turn. "I think I've got it! I can tell which of the two is the guilty one. Jim, you're a genius! We've cracked it!"

To his amazement she strode over to the group of suspects and spoke to each one. Then she took two of them, one after the other, into the barn. When she came out she gave him a thumbs-up sign. She came to back to him and gave another chuckle. "Bingo!" she said. "All I had to do was . . ."

At that moment a whistle sounded and Thorby appeared, summoning them to the gate. "Time's up!" he exclaimed loudly. "Anybody got the answer?"

Several hands went up. "Good, good!" Thorby said. "Right, if you would come forward one by one, please, you can give me you solutions. Who's first?"

Charlotte peered hard at Thorby as he spoke to each candidate and listened to their explanations. Try as she might, she couldn't tell from his expression or gesture whether any of the solutions was acceptable. Her own turn came and she explained as briefly as she could who the murderer was and how she knew. Thorby thanked her non-committally.

When he had spoken to everyone he turned to the group. "Right, chaps," he said, "no point in standing around in the cold. We'll move back to the Three Acorns and get together in a private bar. The landlord has lit a fire for us. Then I'll give you the results. Before we go, a vote of thanks to our gallant volunteers."

Amid scattered applause Thorby handed each of the volunteers a small envelope. They grinned and nodded. One of them went off to collect the Land Rover while another snapped a padlock on the barn. James took Charlotte's arm as they regained the lane. As they walked along she told him about her solution and earned a look of admiration and respect.

Back at the pub Thorby stood pints all round and took up an authoritative position in front of the fire. "Right you are!" he said, "I expect you're eager to hear the results so let's go through them.

"First of all I regret to tell you that not one of you managed to solve the mystery completely. Two people, Charlotte Tamlyn and Dr Sanches Fonseca, scored near misses; congratulations to them. One other, James Ballater, narrowed the suspects down to two. But that was all.

"Most of you thought that the farmer must be the murderer because the tracks in the snow showed that only he could have left the hut after the crime. But if you think about it, that scenario is not logical.

"If he was indeed the criminal he would naturally realise that if he left the tracks as you saw them any detective would immediately focus on him as the prime suspect. He would, therefore, have taken care to obliterate the victim's footprints or trample over them. That would at least divert attention from himself.

"Some of you asked me if I was the murderer. I said that I wasn't, of course. But as I would be permitted to lie that didn't help you. A different question to me would have given you a valuable lead but no one asked it.

"This was the actual plot. The farmer, who was in the conspiracy, *carried* the murderer to the hut in the Land Rover and left him to kill his victim. At the far gate he told his foreman about the body and the foreman left to telephone the police. Meanwhile the murderer, having done the deed, left by means of a pair of stilts. He used them to walk in the heelprints of the victim's trail." A sigh of appreciation swept the room.

"That much could be discovered by a careful examination of the footprints," Thorby went on. "But the suspect had still to be identified. Miss Tamlyn and Dr Fonseca both worked out that each suspect could be asked if the one next to him had used stilts. In the event two answered affirmatively. Man C said that man D had used them and D said the same about C.

Evidently one of these two had to be the murderer. Only Miss Tamlyn actually found which of them it was, although even she didn't spot how he got to the hut in the first place. Perhaps we can ask her how she did it. Miss Tamlyn, would you tell us, please?"

Charlotte rose to her feet, blushing prettily. "Well, it was a bit of a long shot, really," she said. "It occurred to me that if a man was using stilts in the usual way, with his feet on the supports inside the stilt legs, he would find it almost impossible to see how to set the foot of each stilt in a heelmark with precision.

"To do so accurately he would have to rotate the stilts so that the foot supports where sticking outwards. He could then use them with the tops against his shoulders and his feet on the outsides. That way he could see where he was stepping.

"I called the men labelled C and D into the barn separately

and asked them to show me how they walked with the stilts. C used them in the normal way but D put his feet outside them, as I had surmised. So D was the murderer!"

She blushed again as James applauded loudly. "Well done, well done indeed!" Thorby said. "Dr Fonseca followed the same line of reasoning but was honest enough to tell me that he chose D on the off-chance because his shoes were cleaner than C's shoes. That wasn't conclusive, of course. James Ballater narrowed it down to C and D but wasn't able to say which of them was the criminal.

"Well, that's all for this afternoon, ladies and gentlemen. Thank you all very much for taking part. I hope that you have enjoyed your country jaunt and the test itself. Don't call us, as the saying goes. We'll call you next week and let you know who is to be our physiologist. Thanks once again for participating."

James got to his feet and turned to Charlotte. "May I ask a favour?" he said. "I came out here by bus but I see the next one back doesn't arrive for two hours. Could you possibly give me a lift into town?"

Charlotte wondered if he had arranged to travel by bus especially in order to beg a lift. Dismissing the thought as unworthy she agreed to take him into town and was glad she had done so when he proved to be a warm and entertaining companion. They talked and laughed all the way and she was happy to accept his offer of dinner in the evening.

In the course of the meal he became quieter and graver. She asked him if anything was bothering him.

"Well," he said, toying with a dessert fork, "it occurs to me that as you came closest to the test solution you are likely to be chosen to join this expedition. If so, I shan't be seeing you for many months. That's a solemn thought."

Charlotte looked down. "I should be sorry, too," she said.

"But I'll be back in due course. You can keep a place for me in the Royal Orthopaedic or wherever. And you can look at my Matto Grosso photo albums!"

They left it at that and over the next few days James struggled with his dilemma. Deep down he wanted to persuade her not to go to South America but at the same time he didn't want to deprive her of something that she clearly wanted to do. Thorby had apparently disappeared from town and he was unable to find out what Lord Cawston had in mind. Finally he rang up Dr Fonseca, who was the only other person likely to be involved, and chatted to him.

The following Saturday, by appointment, James and Charlotte met in the local park in the shelter of a huge umbrella. A thaw had set in. The paths shone with water and the trees dripped onto them mournfully. Charlotte, however, was all smiles.

"Have you heard from Thorby?" she asked him. "I have. Do you know who's going with the expedition? You'll never guess. It's Dr Fonseca! He showed that he could do well in the initiative test and on top of that he is fluent in Portuguese. So that's that!"

James took her hand in his. "I'm so sorry, Charlotte. You must be disappointed, after doing so well. But I can't say I'm sorry, myself. This'll give us time to develop a few initiatives of our own. If you would care to, that is?"

Charlotte dimpled. "I hope that I pass the test," she said demurely.

"You've already passed, with flying colours," he assured her. There was no need to tell her what he had learned from Dr Fonseca – that she had voluntarily withdrawn her application. Some test results were better kept confidential.

Thanks for the Memory

As the pale silvery light slowly grew brighter he could make out his surroundings. He was sitting in a large field of grass and small coloured plants. Towards the light he could see ragged hedges throwing long cold shadows. The field seemed empty but beside him he found a smooth mauve plastic box a little bigger than his foot, with touch-buttons and a small screen on the top. He looked at it, puzzled.

Off to one side an opening in the hedge revealed a framework of wood leaning wearily from a square post. Beyond it a wide grey path could be glimpsed.

He picked up the box, feeling it might be useful, got to his feet and walked towards the opening. A cold sensation came from behind him and he discovered a patch of wetness on the seat of his shiny suit. He brushed at it with one hand.

As he moved across the field he tried desperately to remember where he was. No matter how hard he concentrated he found he had no idea. He could have been anywhere; all he knew was that he had never been in this field before. He tried to remember how he had come to be there at all but again his memory was blank. With dismay he realised that he didn't even know who he was.

He stepped through the opening in the hedge and found himself on the grey path. In one direction the path sloped down towards some distant buildings set about with bushy trees. To one side was a pond with birds floating on it.

From the other direction he heard a patter of sound. He looked round and saw a man of about his own height walking towards him; he was dressed in rough brown garments and carried a curved stick in his hand. Beside him a small animal bounded along, looking up at the man from time to time.

"Morning!" said the man in brown. "Lovely day, isn't it? I see you're smartly dressed for the country. Where are you off to, then?"

He panicked, not knowing the answer. He opened his mouth to say something and managed only a hesitant sound. The small animal moved forward and sniffed curiously at his legs.

"Haven't made up your mind?" asked the man companionably. "Well, I see you've got your lunch box with you. How about a spot of rabbiting down in the copse there? Good sport, that. Down, Winnie!"

He looked at the box in his hand and wondered if it really contained 'lunch'. Along with everything else, he couldn't remember what was in the box. Perhaps if he opened it the contents would remind him of something. He prodded the button in the middle and the screen on top lit up.

A message appeared on the screen. It read: "Your name is TIMOTHY. The nearest animal to you is a DOG. It is not hostile. There is another man in the ROAD. He has sent you a message about RABBITING and COPSE. Terms not understood. Database search in progress."

He looked up from the screen to the man in brown, who was peering at the box with interest. "Ah, that's one of them hand-held tellies, is it?" he said. "All electrical gadgets these days; I don't know where it's going to end, I'm sure."

Clearly the man was anxious to communicate with him. Perhaps if he responded he could find out where he was and how he had got there. "Morning," he said, as that appeared to be the customary greeting word. "My name is Timothy. I am not hostile to you or your dog. What is your name and the name of this place?"

The man gaped at him in astonishment. Then he appeared to soften and adopted a soothing friendly tone. "Ah, yes. Good morning, Timothy. My name's Ted – Ted Bellinson. I live back at that farmhouse – see it? With the smoke coming out of the chimney? The village down there is called Leythorpe. It's pretty, isn't it? Shall we walk down the hill and have a closer look?"

He took Timothy's arm, turned him and urged him along the road. Timothy was uncertain whether he should go along but he decided that nothing would be lost by learning more about his companion and the locality. Surreptitiously he prodded the button on his box again. The screen presented more text.

"SMOKE is combustion vapour. CHIMNEY is channel for conveying smoke. FARMHOUSE is combination word for dwelling of agricultural people. VILLAGE is group of farmhouses and other buildings in country. Search continues."

Timothy did his best to make a mental note of the terms. As he and Ted strolled down the hill the light in the sky grew brighter still and an amber-coloured sun rose over the distant woods. Winnie barked briefly at a movement in the hedgerow and a bird flew up and away.

"You'll like the village," Ted went on reassuringly. "We'll go and see old Doc Hadlow. He's a nice chap. He'll be able to help you."

Hastily he pushed the button on the box. The screen immediately responded. "DOC is abbreviation for DOCTOR, a man who repairs and maintains people. HELP is service offered by people, usually co-operative but may conceal hostile intent. Clarify."

"Help?" enquired Timothy. "What is help? I do not know if one of your people should help me. Clarify."

Ted glanced at him. "There's a little word called 'please', you know, Timothy. You know what help is, don't you? When somebody makes something easier for you? It's a good thing to help other people, you know. That way we all get along better."

This time the box emitted a faint beep. Timothy looked down at the screen. "RABBITING, artificial word, is finding and killing RABBITS, small furry animals. COPSE is group of trees with undergrowth. PLEASE is indication of courtesy with no specific meaning. Help not clarified; obtain more information."

"Tell me more about help," Timothy said. "Is 'spot of rabbiting' something to help me? It involves killing. If you kill me will we get along together – please?"

Ted's expression became grim and he compressed his lips. "Never you mind, Timothy," he said quietly. "We won't go rabbiting if you don't want to. Let's go and find Doc Hadlow. He can help you. Help is good for you, you see if it isn't."

They had arrived at the first of the houses and Ted steered him towards a small building with a sign outside saying SURGERY and other words. Ted put his finger on a button; there was no screen with a message but Timothy heard the sound of a bell somewhere inside. Ted called Winnie to his side and told her to sit.

After a few moments a muscular female figure in a blue and white dress opened a door in the wall. She nodded to Ted and waited.

"Sorry to bother you so early, Mrs Hadlow," Ted said, "but I wonder if the doc could take a look at this chap. Says his name's Timothy. I found him wandering up at Sevenacres; he seems a bit confused like."

The woman glanced at Timothy and then stood back and motioned them to enter. They went into a room with small frameworks round the walls and sat on two of them. Timothy's box identified them as chairs. The woman disappeared while Winnie curled up on the floor and snoozed.

Timothy stared at piles of shiny coloured papers on a low table. For some time nothing happened. Timothy wondered if the doc had decided not to give him the help service; he must obtain more information.

Then another door with a frosted glass panel opened and a man in a white coat appeared. He exchanged a few mumbled words with Ted and then made a gesture to Timothy, inviting him into the next room.

Timothy followed him into the room, which was equipped with a number of strange objects. There were cabinets with bottles and jars. In one corner he saw the bony framework of a man without any flesh hanging from a metal rod. It frightened him. The man in the white coat turned to him with a pleasant look.

"Hallo, I'm Doctor Hadlow. And you're Timothy, are you? Have you got another name? No? Just Timothy? All right, Timothy, where do you live? Round here?"

His box gave one of its beeps; he was learning how it operated. He put it on the flat surface beside him and consulted the screen. It read, "Answer: 'No, I come from a distant place. What is your intention?'"

"I – I come from a distant place," he told the doctor. "What is your intention? Are you hostile? Please." At least his memory was good enough to remember the courtesy word, he thought.

Dr Hadlow glanced at the box and smiled in a kindly fashion. "Now, Timothy, of course I'm not hostile to you," he said. "There's no need to be afraid. But I think you're rather confused about things, aren't you? Perhaps I can help you. I'm just going to examine you and then we'll decide what to do next. All right?"

But despite Dr Hadlow's amicable demeanour Timothy

became more and more alarmed over the next few minutes. The doctor put a tube in each ear and brought out various pieces of equipment; he appeared to be measuring Timothy's heat, eye sensors and bodily sounds. As he did so his eyes widened in disbelief and he peered at Timothy with shock and incredulity.

"Ye gods!" Timothy heard him mutter. "That's impossible!" He turned to him again and spoke in a normal tone. "Listen, Timothy, you're in a – a bit of a state. Your temperature and heart rate are, shall we say, not exactly what they should be. Not at all. In fact they might be dangerous to you.

"Now, what I'm going to do, I'm going to give you a small injection to make you feel better and more relaxed. Do you understand? It won't hurt you – you'll just feel a little pinprick, that's all. Then afterwards you'll be calmer and not so confused."

He turned to one of the cabinets on the wall and took out a small instrument with a sharp point on one end. He inserted it into a tiny bottle and held it up in front of the window so that Timothy could see it clearly. The familiar beep sounded.

"Man is holding a SYRINGE," read the screen on the box. "Syringe can be used as weapon. Deduction: intention is hostile. Do not make contact with syringe."

Timothy backed away from the doctor, leaving his box on the desk. "Do not help me with your syringe," he said. "Syringe and rabbiting are hostile. I wish to communicate with Ted and Winnie. Please!"

"In a few minutes," replied Dr Hadlow gently. "First we must make you feel better." He pressed a push-button on his desk. The door behind Timothy opened and, at a nod from the doctor, he felt his arms being gripped from behind by the woman who had answered the front door.

The doctor advanced towards him and Timothy found, to his alarm, that he could not break away from the woman behind him. He struggled and twisted but her grip was implacable. He looked despairingly at his plastic box and saw a tiny brilliant light flashing from a corner of the screen.

In the waiting room Winnie looked up suddenly and growled. Ted heard an ear-splitting crack and saw a blinding flash of light through the frosted glass. He rushed over and threw the door open.

In the consulting room he found Dr Hadlow, with syringe poised, facing his wife who was standing near the other door with open hands raised. Timothy was nowhere to be seen.

The three looked at each other in stunned horror. Before anyone could speak the box on the doctor's desk emitted a low beep. They hesitated, exchanging another look; then Ted and the doctor went cautiously across to look at the screen. A message was outlined on it.

"ALERT! Hostile action detected. Android explorer has been retracted to command centre. Explorer will return when Earth information has been analysed. Portable memory scanner will be retracted within FIVE Earth minutes. END."

Turning a New Loaf

IT HAD been an exhausting week in the insurance office secretarial pool. Lynn sat and stared at the word-processing screen in front of her. On Friday afternoons her fingers didn't seem to go where her brain sent them. She had just asked a customer: 'Are you sure you have enough wife assurance?'

Perhaps it wasn't only Fridays. The previous week she had addressed a major supplier as 'Dead Sir'. Marjorie, the pool supervisor, had not been amused.

Luckily it was an internal memo in which she had urged her friend Rosie to 'turn over a new loaf'. She had sent it direct from her screen through the communications net so Marjorie hadn't spotted it. Still, it could only be a matter of time before the next typo reared its tiny head.

She thought again about Rosie. As her best friend Rosie was lively and stimulating. She cared little for her appearance and even less for other people's opinions on it but she was always good company.

However although Rosie was casual and untidy to the point of exasperation Lynn had to admit that her keyboard output was immaculate, with every indented paragraph marshalled and every comma in place. The Friday syndrome didn't seem to affect her.

She and Rosie had joined the firm on the same day nearly a year ago and had stuck up an immediate alliance. They liked the same snack food, wandered round the same department stores and exchanged the latest singles. They even met their respective boyfriends together, in the saloon bar of The Brindled Ferret.

At first Derek and Simon had made up a quartet with them. It was fun to go around as a group, laughing at old photograph albums, shrieking encouragement at motocross meetings and grabbing corner tables at hamburger joints and discos. Derek, tall and neatly dressed, made a good foil for good-natured Simon in his corduroys and rough check shirts.

Gradually, however, their relationships altered. She and Derek became quieter and more reserved with each other. He treated her with a poise and deference that she found appealing. They discussed drama and poetry. He was obviously attracted to her but he didn't try to push their friendship along too fast. She liked that.

The others were altogether different. Simon was, if possible, even more happy-go-lucky than Rosie. He took nothing seriously. His comments and opinions were delivered in a series of one-liners. He was a mine of information on Arsenal and Sting but beyond those topics his philosophy evaporated.

Only yesterday Rosie had shyly confided in Lynn that she fancied Simon with an aching intensity but Simon didn't seem to be aware of it. He was all quick-fire banter and made no effort to be alone with her. A drink, a laugh and a wave of the hand and he was off until their next rendezvous.

"I might as well be his sister," Rosie complained. "He always seems glad to see me but he never asks how I've been or what I'd like to do at the weekend. In fact I've only had one telephone call from him and that was to say he couldn't make a date we had arranged. I don't believe he thinks about me at all."

"Oh, I'm sure he does," Lynn said. "He was saying to Derek and me only the other day how much fun you were. He did, truly!"

"Yeah, I'm just a bundle of laughs," said Rosie glumly. "That's the trouble. He doesn't take me seriously. Have you noticed – he never holds a door open for me like your Derek? He just waves me on and smirks 'After you – the punk before the hunk!'"

"Yes, well, you don't exactly make it easy for him, do you, Rosie?"

"Make it easy? What does he want, a diagram? Simon's been around; if he wants to play the game he knows what the moves are."

Lynn sighed. "That's just it, Rosie. A relationship is not a game. There shouldn't be a winner and a loser, just two winners – you know what I mean? The way you look and behave he's probably afraid of being the loser."

"What do you mean, the way I look? I always look the same – what you see is what you get!"

"Maybe he doesn't want to get what he sees," Lynn said drily. "A man doesn't necessarily want to put his arm round a bundle wrapped in torn jeans and a leather jacket with a wrinkled picture of Alice Cooper on the back. Not to mention the metal CND and Save the Whales badges. There are times when he might feel like cuddling something softer and silkier and scented, if you follow me."

Rosie pondered for a moment. "Not my lifestyle," she said. "I'm not your femme fatale, more your good time gal. I just don't have the face or the hair or the figure to fascinate the male of the species."

"Don't be silly, of course you have!" Lynn exclaimed. "But you might think about – how can I put it? – a new image. You know, a fresh approach. A change is as good as a rest, so they say. It might work wonders."

Rosie said nothing more but Lynn noticed her thoughtful

expression. Clearly she was in planning mode. That evening she was less boisterous with Simon and he seemed more attentive than usual.

Today, Friday, Lynn noticed several other things. First, in the lunch hour Rosie bought herself some blue eye shadow, although Lynn knew she never used eye shadow. Then when she got back to the office she made some mysterious telephone calls; Lynn heard her saying, ". . . got to be brand new – that's important!"

Later she insisted on borrowing fifteen pounds from Lynn without explanation, although it was the end of the month and everybody had just received their salary. Finally Lynn caught her picking something out of her waste-paper basket and stuffing it into her purse. She recognised Rosie's diary for the previous year.

"What do you want that for?" Lynn enquired. "That's past history. Or are you writing an article on your meteoric career in insurance?"

"Might do!" Rosie smiled. "I could call it A Change of Policy. You know why? Look, I've decided to take your advice. Like you said in your note, I'm going to turn over a new loaf – or did you mean leaf?" She laughed and winked. "It's all change for Rosie – a new life, starting tomorrow!"

Lynn gave her a quizzical look. "I take it that this new life has something to do with Simon?" she said quietly.

"Sort of. Anyway, the thing is, tomorrow's the day. Tomorrow I'm going to *do it!*"

"What do you mean, do it? Do what? Rosie, what are you cooking up?"

"Never you mind. Don't worry, you'll know all about it. But I want it to be a surprise."

Lynn felt a twinge of alarm. "Rosie, when you said you're going to – to do it, what did you mean? You're not going to 'do it' with Simon, are you? Rosie, don't be a fool! Stop and think!"

Rosie raised her eyebrows and looked knowing. "I don't know what you mean," she said. "What are you getting at?"

Lynn felt like shaking her. "Tell me! Before you go any further. Are you thinking of . . .?" Her nerve failed her. "Are you going to – to move in with him, or something?"

Rosie tossed her head and smiled tantalisingly. "Wait and see!" she said. "Actually, you won't have too long to wait. Come round at four-thirty tomorrow afternoon and all will be revealed. All right?"

Lynn could get nothing further out of her. Whatever Rosie had in mind she wasn't going to offer any clues.

That evening in the saloon bar Lynn dumped the problem in Derek's capable hands. She had faith in Derek's cool consideration and his ability to think his way through a puzzle. Rosie's odd behaviour and her own doubts and fears came tumbling out.

"Well, there it is!" she told him. "Rosie is determined to do something drastic tomorrow, no doubt about it. Giddy or not, when she makes up her mind to do something nothing will shake her. She's been acting strangely all week but where Simon comes into it I don't know. Any ideas?"

Derek took a pull at his pint of bitter and frowned slightly in concentration. "Let's begin with the strange incidents earlier on," he said. "You say she ordered something new over the phone and borrowed some money from you that she didn't need?"

"Yes, and she got that blue eye shadow – something she's never used in her life! And then she grabbed that useless old diary and hid it away. Somehow it looked a bit guilty to me."

"Hm! There must be a link. What is it? An old diary and something brand new over the phone. That's a contrast. And why the borrowed money . . .? Aha! Of course! It stares you in the face! Why didn't we see it straight away?"

"Don't be infuriating, Derek! It doesn't stare me in the face. What's the explanation?"

Derek grinned. "Something every girl knows. Don't you see what she was collecting? Something old, something new, something borrowed . . ."

"Something blue! The eye shadow, of course. Small enough to carry, like the diary." She sat up in shock. "But that's impossible, Derek! She can't be getting married tomorrow. Without telling me, her best friend? It's unthinkable! And anyway Simon would have said something to you about being best man and all that."

Derek pursed his lips and studied the table top. "Unless, of course, they felt that they – er – had to get married quietly," he suggested.

"No, Derek, I can't believe it. They're not on anything like such intimate terms. I know because Rosie told me she would have liked to be closer but Simon apparently wasn't too interested.

"In any case why the secrecy? They haven't given anyone a chance to give them wedding presents. And another thing – Rosie is in the office next week working on those foreign policy renewals so they won't be having a honeymoon either."

"Maybe not, but didn't she say all would be revealed tomorrow afternoon? It's obvious, I'd say. That gives them time to get back from the registry office and offer us some cake and bubbly. We'd better dress up a bit."

Lynn went home in a sombre mood. Derek was taking the whole thing lightly, she thought. He had refused to contact Simon so she spent the next morning telephoning some of their office friends for more information. No one could tell her anything.

Finally at lunch time in desperation she rang Rosie's number. Her mother answered. No, Rosie wasn't in, but she would be back later in the afternoon, with Simon. Could she take a message?

Apart from something like 'It's your funeral, girl!' Lynn could think of nothing useful to say. She put the phone down in a fit of bafflement and pique.

At half-past four on the dot she and Derek presented themselves at Rosie's door. Her mother let them in with a mysterious smile and gestured towards the front room.

They went in, to find Simon collapsed in a armchair with a look of awe and wonder on his face. Standing close by him with her back to them was an ash-blonde girl in a crisp cocktail dress, holding a wine glass in her manicured fingertips.

She turned on one elegant shoe and Lynn gasped. "Rosie! What on earth . . .?"

Rosie tried a haughty pose, then giggled and reached out a hand to draw her closer. "Well, what do you think?" she said, giving a slow twirl. "It was your idea, you know. A new image, you said. Sorry I had to borrow some money but I couldn't wait. I telephoned to get an appointment at Curl Up & Dye on the way home and had to pay them cash."

"Rosie, you look fabulous, doesn't she, Simon? The eye shadow suits you and the blond tint. But it was wicked of you not to tell me. I've worried myself sick wondering what you were up to. Go on, show us the ring!"

"Ring? What ring?" Rosie said, flashing a sideways glance and frowning a warning.

"So you aren't . . . I mean, we thought that you . . . Well, anyway, that explains the loan and the new look. It's terrific. But I'm dying to know – what was the old diary for?"

Rosie looked down at Simon. "I thought Simon might like a reminder of the old me," she said, "just in case the change didn't work out. But I think he likes the new loaf."

Simon reached out and pulled her down onto his lap. "Best thing since sliced bread," he said happily.

Double Invention

When the fishing fleet was in, Valerie loved the little Portuguese port of Cascais. While the nearby city of Lisbon was fascinating with its old castle and pavement cafés, the port area offered only rusting cranes and the heavy smell of oil. However she could always reach Cascais by the swift electric train that took the football fans to Cruz Quebrada and the roulette addicts to Estoril.

Strolling round Cascais harbour Valerie was always intrigued by the contrasts in the unfolding scene. On one side of her, sleek powerful Atlantic combers thundered against the outside of the harbour wall, opening sudden fans of spray. The plaints of the soaring gulls and the salt-sour smell of seaweed assailed her; they combined with the vista of heaving sea to create both a stirring picture and, later, a clear image on the screen of her nostalgia.

On the other side all was calm. Lobster pots were piled in haphazard fashion against the breakwater and fishing nets were spread out to dry all over the place. Small colourful dinghies danced gently at their moorings and in the distance a mauve backdrop of wooded hills smiled down.

Valerie first noticed Marco among the Portuguese fishermen in their rough jerseys and knitted caps. The misty spray from the breakers drifted across the quay but the fishermen, unheeding, made an animated group against the wet grey stone as they tossed baskets of *sardinhas* up to the top of the wall by her feet.

She heard Marco's name when the others called to him to catch a thrown line or a creel of *bacalhau*. He was evidently a crew member from one of the boats but somehow he looked a little different from the other men. Unlike the usual Portuguese black, his hair was dark brown and his face was not shaven blue but tanned and rosy. His eyes were brown, as she discovered when he glanced up at her.

"Hallo, there!" he said in Portuguese. "Like some fresh shrimp for tea? Wait a minute and you can have some." His metropolitan accent was a cut above the normal rough speech of the fisherfolk. Having studied the language in both England and Brazil Valerie had an ear for accents.

The unloading finished soon afterwards and Marco joined her on the quay with an athletic leap. He poured a double handful of shrimps and *pescados* into a plastic bag and handed it to her with mock formality. "Here you are, they're delicious!" he said. "Now, what about a *galão*?"

Valerie knew that a *galão* was a milky coffee served in a glass, so it seemed safe to accept. They found a quayside café and sat under a striped awning, sipping and chatting. Fearless herring gulls strutted between the tables picking up old crusts and other scraps. Donkeys with woolly ear-tassels passed by on the cobbles, loaded with panniers.

Marco was easy to talk to; soon she was telling him all about her upbringing in England and her family's move to Brazil, where she had attended high school for a year. She told him about her return to a job in England and her decision to take this holiday in the Lisbon area, aided by her familiarity with the language. "Although really it's colloquial Brazilian," she apologised. "What I need is conversation practice in Portugal."

"At your service," he twinkled. "Let's begin here and now!" But although he chattered away nineteen to the dozen, teaching her the diminutives and contractions that the local people used in their everyday speech, she became aware that he revealed very little about his own family and himself. He appeared to have a brother called Silvio but that was all. His reserve seemed to be at variance with his open nature; she wondered what he was hiding from her.

Over the next two weeks they explored the area. They admired the flowering plants in the *estufa fria*, took the lift to the top of the huge statue of Christ across the estuary and drove out to Sintra to tour the palace and chaffer for glazed pots in the local market. On other days she met him at Cascais and they ate intimate candle-lit suppers and laughed at his jokes in low tones.

Valerie realised that she was becoming absorbed in him. She couldn't get his winning smile and attentive gestures out of her mind. Her impending departure grew from a matter of regret to an onrushing dread, scarcely to be imagined.

She mustn't get involved, she decided. Guiltily she invented a 'friend', by implication a fiancé in England, to whom she would be returning in a few days, at the end of her holiday.

Marco's manner was warm and affectionate by now but he made no move to draw her close. His brown eyes spoke volumes but his actual words, though informal, were unfailingly polite. He did not presume to address her as *tu*, the more intimate form of 'you'. And always his home and background remained a mystery, apart from brother Silvio who never made an appearance.

Maybe, Valerie thought, it was for the best after all. A romantic entanglement would be difficult for both of them. Their lives were lived in different worlds: cosmopolitan London and quaint, simple Cascais, preoccupied with tourism and the current price of fish. She sighed, thinking of the TAP aircraft that would soon fly her from one world to the other with finality.

The shock came the very next day. For once, Valerie was

waiting for Marco on the inside of their favourite café, having found that the letter she intended to leave him kept blowing away from the outside table in the sea breeze.

All at once she heard his familiar voice and looked up, but he was evidently sitting under the outer awning with a companion. She half rose; then she heard his words and realised with a start that they were in perfect English.

"Listen, Philip, I've met this smashing girl. Valerie, her name is. She's tremendous – everything I ever wanted! She's attractive, she's intelligent – gorgeous figure, too. I'm mad about her!"

A deeper voice replied. "Then why don't you do something about it? What's the problem?"

"The usual, I'm afraid. She's already got someone in England, damn his eyes. She's going back to him in a couple of days, just before I have to go back myself. It's no good – I'm too late. I gather from the odd remark that they're practically engaged."

"My dear Mark," said the other voice, "it's not like you to wallow in self-pity. Go on, tell her how you feel. What have you got to lose? Woo her. Go for it, man!"

Valerie's head was spinning. So his name was Mark! And he wasn't a local fisherman – he was going back to England! She sat frowning down at her farewell note. Why hadn't he spoken earlier? What was the mystery? And how on earth was she going to talk to him when they met in a few minutes?

Without warning he entered the café with an empty glass and saw her. Instantly, realising that he'd been overheard, he crossed to her and took her hands.

"Oh Lord, Valerie, I've been such a fool! When you came across me helping the fishermen I thought you were a Portuguese girl. Later on, when you told me about yourself and wanted to practise the local lingo I thought it might embarrass you to switch to English. So I just carried on as we were.

Double Invention

"Incidentally, my father is English but Mum's Portuguese. That's why I'm here; I'm visiting my grandmother. I didn't tell you, of course."

Many things were becoming clear to Valerie. She heard his next words dimly, in a whirl of emotion.

"I'm sorry you heard me talking to Philip just now. You did, didn't you? Well, actually, I'm not sorry in a way. It's helped me to explain everything, which is what I was wanting to do. But don't worry, I won't bother you in England. I'll just fade out. That's the best thing. By the way, Silvio doesn't exist; I'm afraid I made him up."

Valerie smiled with relief and gripped his hands. "No bother," she murmured. "Don't worry about the fiancé. I made *him* up as well."

On with the New

As Elizabeth rounded the corner of the house and started down the side path she saw Vincent standing quietly near the garden shed. He seemed to be chewing on something, as usual, but was otherwise motionless in the bright morning sunlight.

Elizabeth hadn't expected to find him there at this hour. She hesitated for a moment, not relishing the encounter, and then moved resolutely on. After all, why should she let Vincent put her off her walk?

She considered ignoring him altogether but decided that it would be too obvious – melodramatic, even. Better to behave as neutrally as possible. She nodded casually as she approached him and even managed a noncommittal "Hallo, Vincent," as she hurried by.

Vincent looked at her, rather longingly she thought, and lifted his head a little as though contemplating a response. However he made no move to join her and she heard no sound from him as she unlatched the back gate. She passed through, closing the gate with a deep click, and strode on across the pasture, first following a beaten path towards the stream and then wandering over to the little copse.

It was a favourite walk of hers, brushing through the tall grasses and avoiding the occasional clump of thistles. Among the blades of grass she could see pale sprays of allium and yellow heads of calendula swaying in the breeze. Somewhere further off a meadow lark sang.

Elizabeth remembered, with a pang of regret, how she and Vincent had once explored the rolling fields and woods together. They had found new tracks and bridle-paths, many of them overgrown, and come upon streams and coverts the existence of which Elizabeth, who had lived there all her life, had not suspected. It was like journeying into a new but strangely familiar land, with the added delight of sharing the discovery with a close partner.

For in those days they had been inseparable. Each had seemed to complement the other, enjoying the same pursuits and taking pleasure in each other's company. She found in Vincent a source of strength and wanted no other companion. She knew that he enjoyed their forays as much as she did.

She sighed. Things were different now. Vincent's manner was outwardly the same and his behaviour was as correct as it had always been. In fact his good manners had been one of the things that attracted her to him from the beginning. She was sure that if she gave him some encouragement he would be as open and friendly as before.

Elizabeth felt a glum sense of remorse. She faced the fact that she would not be encouraging Vincent or even consoling him, if indeed consolation would help. Her regret deepened to guilt as she contemplated the change in their relationship and the reason for it. In truth, it was her fault.

She scrambled across a dry ditch, treacherous with nettles, and entered the copse. Leaves rustled and shifted under her feet; here and there clumps of fern stood close like gossiping friends and in a glade further off a theatrical shaft of sunlight fell diagonally, as onto a stage. The cooler air greeted her legs and a small animal scampered away to the safety of a pollarded beech.

She had often come to the calm of the wood to think and today she took a grip on herself and faced the situation with Vincent squarely. Yes, it was her fault and Daniel's.

Daniel was merely the cause, the unexpected entrant on the scene, the new term in the equation. Daniel would surely have been shocked and hurt if he could have suspected that he had somehow come between two others. But he didn't.

Elizabeth had revealed nothing of her feelings to Daniel, either when they first saw each other or later. She had met him for the first time at the local agricultural show two days ago and was interested in an instant.

She couldn't speak to him among the crowd of farmers and holiday-makers but she spent some time near the roped-off area where he was sauntering up and down, perhaps waiting for someone. For a brief moment their eyes actually met and she imagined a gleam of interest in his gaze. Or was it imagination? Before she left she was taken with him.

Yesterday she had returned to the show, ostensibly to buy seeds for the garden but in reality, she had to admit, to catch another glimpse of Daniel. She actually strolled aimlessly across his path at one point but this time he didn't appear to notice her. Her eyes followed him and she was appalled to find that she wanted to be near him, to offer him little gifts, to brush his brown wind-blown hair out of his eyes.

Once upon a time, she remembered, she had wanted to do the same for Vincent and had even thought of making him a loose garment or something of the kind. Never, though, had she felt such a strong caring impulse as she did now.

That evening, finding that she couldn't get Daniel out of her mind, she saw that she needed help. Her father was a bluff and genial man, wise in the ways of the world and always abreast of the latest developments in the county. As a member of the show's organising committee he might even know something of Daniel's background.

She mused. Father's counsel would be practical and to the point, she knew. He would not be swayed by Daniel's appealing character, still less his looks. He would talk seriously about judging a book by its cover, about loyalty to Vincent and about the solid moral principles which had guided his life and which he would commend to his family.

Elizabeth loved her father but she instinctively recognised that her present problem lay outside the wide circle of his goodness and common sense. That recognition was tinged with the suspicion that his advice might not be quite what she wanted to hear. She squirmed. Did she truly want sound advice or was it conspiratorial sympathy she was after?

She had gone to find her mother. Helen was sitting peeling onions into a bowl in the kitchen; the errant tears on her cheeks seemed to anticipate Elizabeth's trouble and promise a warm and ready solution. She put an arm round her mother's slim waist and looked over her shoulder at the glistening onions.

"Mum, I've got a problem!" she blurted out, and stopped. How could she describe her emotions so as to make her dilemma clear? Her mother, she was sure, had never had to cope with sudden yearnings or been bothered by such things as divided loyalties. All her life Elizabeth had never known her to dither or appear flustered. She was the embodiment of virtue and fidelity.

Helen put down her knife and swished her fingers in the bowl. "Don't look so distraught, dear," she said calmly. "What is the problem? It may not be as hopeless as you think. Can I do anything?"

Elizabeth leaned against her mother in relief and poured out her story. She tried to hold nothing back. She acknowledged her fondness for Vincent from the time he had come to stay with them. Then she described Daniel and how the sight of him had driven everything else from her mind.

"What shall I do, Mummy? I don't want to drive Vincent away but I couldn't bear to lose Daniel, before we even . . . It's the last day of the show tomorrow and he'll be gone!" She coloured and summoned her strength. "It's awful but I – I want him!"

Helen picked up a tea towel and dried her hands on it absently. "Gently, darling," she said. "There's no need to dash into something you may regret. Why don't you get to know Daniel before anything else? You can have him here, if you like. And remember, you don't cast aside an old friend just because you've found a new one. Think about it."

Elizabeth had thought, practically ever since. Now, here among the cool lofty trees, she came to a decision. It would be heartless to the point of cruelty to dismiss Vincent, worthy trusting Vincent, after all they had done together. He would stay, and welcome.

But that afternoon she would go back to the showground and collect Daniel, if he was still for sale, to delight her eyes and reward her care. The two ponies could share the paddock and become friends; all three of them would be part of one contented family.

Two's Company

THE cafeteria was hot and crowded. Alison paid the cashier, picked up her tray from the long shiny counter and turned. A flickering sea of faces and hands confronted her, eating, drinking, talking, reaching, gesticulating. The hubbub beat upon her ears.

At that moment a family rose from a table in the far corner and made for the exit, the mother shepherding a small girl while father marched importantly behind. Alison gratefully made her way across the room, only to come to a stop halfway, feeling a little foolish.

In her haste she had forgotten to collect a sachet of sugar from the box at the end of the counter, to say nothing of a teaspoon and paper napkin. Well, it had been a long day, she reflected.

She looked round uncertainly. Should she go back for the missing items, breasting the tide of incoming customers, some of whom might take the vacated chairs? She weighed the risk and decided to continue towards her goal. On reaching the corner table she swept aside the used plates and cutlery, deposited her tray and went back across the room.

Returning from the counter she noticed that someone had indeed occupied one of the other chairs at the table. She studied his profile as best she cold while negotiating a path through the crowd.

It was exactly the kind of face she liked, with a firm jawline, a kindly tilt to the mouth and unruly chestnut hair with little glints at the ends. His shoulders looked square set in a smart dark blue blazer. She dropped her gaze as she slid into her chair and concentrated on tearing a corner off the little sachet.

"You don't mind?" he said courteously, with a small open-handed gesture indicating his own presence at the table.

"Not at all," she responded with equal civility, taking the opportunity to glance at him full face. He was rugged rather than handsome, with keen grey eyes and the humorous twist to the mouth now fully revealed.

The eyes appraised her while he arranged a cake and two biscuits on a plate. He leaned forward slightly to say something else but was cut off by a high-pitched voice over their heads.

"Whoo, found a place at last! What a scrum, eh? This isn't taken, is it? No? Thank the Lord for that!"

A third tray descended, followed by a round-shouldered gnome of a man, who didn't so much take his seat as fall into it like a pile of wet laundry. He beamed at them cheerily through thick brass-rimmed glasses and ran the back of one hand across a roughly shaven chin. Alison noticed his dark rough-edged cardigan and matching finger nails.

"Had a job finding this place," he confided, picking up a sandwich tightly wrapped in cling film and studying it.

"I'm from the other side of town, see? Had to search this area. Nowhere else to eat for miles. And when you do find a bit of a snack it's a puzzle to get at it." He plopped a straw into a styrofoam beaker and picked at the sandwich wrapping, making little impression.

"But then all of life's a puzzle, isn't it? Don't you think so? Yeah, it's a puzzle all right." He managed to break into the sandwich and beamed at them again, unperturbed by their lack of response.

"When I say a puzzle I don't mean one of those children's riddles. They're just playing with words, really. I mean something you've got to cogitate over. Yeah, cogitate." He seemed to like the flavour of the word. "Do you like puzzles?"

Alison realised that the little man had taken them for a couple and had decided that some ice needed to be broken. She and her companion exchanged a look. He turned back politely to the newcomer and made the error of offering an opening. "Some puzzles can be entertaining," he said quietly, "but on the whole . . ."

The gnome was in like a flash. "Entertaining?" he said. "Here, I'll tell you about a puzzle I came across only yesterday. A real-life puzzle, too, not one from a book. A railway puzzle. This'll entertain you!" He bounced in his seat with relish and took a bite of the sandwich, talking round the mouthful with gusto.

"Listen, yesterday I and a friend of mine from the photographic club had to go over to Ennisdale reservoir. You know Ennisdale? You can get a through ticket but you have to change at Corringham Junction. Actually it's not too bad. At least you can get something in the snack bar while you're waiting. No queue. Not like here!"

He paused for another bite as they watched him, fascinated. He *would* be a fanatical photographer, thought Alison; he had that lone look about him despite the emphasis on the accompanying friend. What did they call them – twitchers?

"Well now, here's the puzzle," he went on, gulping a mouthful down. "On the way to Ennisdale my friend and I noticed that we arrived at Corringham on platform one and had to change to platform two to catch the Ennisdale train. We changed from one to two, got it?

"But on the way back in the evening, the train *from* Ennisdale came in to platform one and, blow me, we had to change to platform two to get our train back here. Same as in the morning, one to two, see?"

He leaned back complacently to judge their surprise until an anxious thought struck him. "I say, you don't happen to know Corringham Junction well, do you?"

He looked from one of them to the other; Alison's neighbour once again stepped into the breach. "Well, actually I do visit Ennisdale now and again but we – that is, I generally go by car." Alison suppressed a smile at the correction.

"Right, well, there's the puzzle. Two journeys, in opposite directions, with all the trains running normally – for once! – but in each case we had to change platforms in the same direction at the junction. One to two each time. How do you account for that, eh?"

He finished the last of the sandwich and drained the beaker with a noise like a washing machine emptying itself. "Puzzling, isn't it?" he said. "Shall I tell you? Do you give up?"

They nodded, as though by prior agreement, to all three questions.

"Well, you see, it's like this. How can I explain it?" He snatched the straw he had been using, slit half of it lengthways with a grubby thumb nail and laid it on the table, bending the slit halves away from each other in curves like the feelers of an insect.

"See, the railway comes from the city to Corringham Junction and then divides, with trains serving both this town and Ennisdale. There are only the two platforms at the junction – that's why they're numbered one and two. Ha, ha!

"All the up trains to the city are on platform one and all the down trains, to both towns, stop at platform two. So if you're travelling between the towns, rather than to the city, you always change the same way, one to two. *Voilà!*"

He peered intently at them, as if uncertain whether the complexity of British Rail's arrangements had been too much for them. Then he crumpled the straw and the cling film into the beaker, gave them a final beam and disappeared as if an invisible conjuror had snapped his fingers. Alison's companion turned to her with a gleeful smile.

"Well, follow that!" he chuckled. "At least you now know how to change trains at Corringham Junction. And what sort of day have you had at the office?"

Alison raised an eyebrow coolly. "How do you know I work in an office?" she asked.

He grimaced, then leaned across and put a warm hand on her knee. "Alison, darling, it was a great idea but let's not go on with this romantic re-run of our first meeting. This place is a lot busier these days. Too many intruders. I'd rather we were alone somewhere on our anniversary."

Alison clasped his hand. "Lead on, darling," she smiled. "And by the way, I'm glad I married you and not a shutterbug. No puzzle about that!"

Noticeable Errors

As Linda collected the glasses from our alcove table in the Scythe & Partridge Charles raised his newly-delivered pewter pot and cocked an eye at us. "Let us greet the new round with a new topic," he said gravely, exactly as he might have intoned 'Let us pray!'

Percy, the amateur psephologist, and Gene, our friendly American journalist, exchanged glances. I could see that they were not used to having a discussion text handed out as if from a pulpit. I inspected my bitter and waited for the pronouncement.

"Let us," said Charles, "examine the state of public English – as distinct, that is, from private English. I fear for the health of public English."

Percy dutifully supplied the response to this bidding prayer. "What do you mean, public English? Is that what we're speaking here, in the pub?"

"No, no!" said Charles. "I am talking about the sort of English that is intended for public consumption, as opposed to the kind we use among ourselves, in gossip and correspondence and so on."

"You mean formal English?" said Gene. "There's nothing new to say about that, is there? We all know about the headmaster writing his Notice to Parents. He can't bring himself to say 'If it rains the prize-giving ceremony will take place in the gym.' He has to climb aboard his pomposity and invoke the ritual 'In case of inclement weather . . .'"

Charles smiled briefly. "I wasn't thinking so much of formal English," he said. "That, I agree, is ground that is not only well trodden but well picked over. No, I'm interested in public notices and announcements – and in how many of them are ambiguous or misleading or just plain wrong.

"The worst offenders seem to be those on the public highway; the writer is so anxious to economise on words that he tends to forget the message that he's trying to convey. And very often he doesn't achieve the desired economy either. Which is more helpful to the lost driver – an English sign reading No Access to Hilltop Crescent or an American one telling him Wrong Way?

"I came across a more subtle example this afternoon. You know the new hospital up on the main road? Well, someone has put up a notice outside it: Silent Zone. That's difficult to believe in a busy town like this. It suggests a cemetery rather than a hospital; not a happy comparison.

"What the notice refers to, presumably, is a zone in which quietness is desired or adjured or simply prevalent. It should, of course, read Silence Zone. Or, better still, No Noise Please."

Gene gave a doubtful twist to his mouth. "Silence Zone? A fine point," he said deliberatively. "If you're going to be that pedantic I imagine you would object to the familiar Trespassers Will Be Prosecuted?" Charles looked at him warily, suspecting levity. "Surely you would want it to say Apprehended Trespassers Will Be Prosecuted?"

Charles inclined his head appreciatively. "Indeed, indeed! A little more apprehension of prosecution wouldn't go amiss! But, as you say, these distinctions are rather fine. Let us descend to the level of more common errors. Suppose you light a cigarette on the lower deck of a bus. The conductor will doubtless point to a notice: No Smoking Allowed. Is he on good ground?"

"Well, I suppose . . ."

"No, he isn't," Charles went on, rhetorically. "More of a burning deck! What the notice tells us is that No Smoking is a permitted state. No smoking is allowed. In other words you may refrain from smoking if you wish. It doesn't tell us whether the act of smoking is allowed or not. Therefore you can puff away!"

"Until an inspector waves the by-laws at you," observed Percy. "You want the notice to say Smoking Not Allowed, I take it. I wonder if there is a notice in any library stating No Reading Aloud? That would puzzle some people, I should think.

"But let's get back to the highway that you mentioned earlier. I seem to remember a case in which a motorist was charged with a parking offence. In court, the traffic warden or policewoman or whoever it was testified that he had left his car under a street sign which stated in large letters: No Parking Both Sides.

"The motorist advanced an impeccable defence. It wasn't you, was it, Charles? He pointed out that he hadn't parked on both sides; he had parked on only one side! Thanking him, the magistrate conceded that the sign should properly have read: No Parking Either Side. He expressed the hope that the £40 fine would be used to repaint it!"

Gene chuckled. "These parking stories are legion. Did you hear about the Canadian who left his car at a well-known beauty spot, only to be prosecuted for a parking offence? When he was asked in court if he had *quelque chose à dire* – anything to say – he protested indignantly that an official sign at the beauty spot proclaimed: Fine for Parking!"

"Not an *amende honorable*," I suggested. "More of a *fine* distinction!" The others groaned ritually. "No doubt the judge was unimpressed, especially if he was a *Quebecois*. Incidentally, how should the sign have been worded? Penalty for Parking Law Violation sounds pretty heavy."

"But less heavily ambiguous," said Charles. "Most of these errors arise from the fact that the writer of the sign is looking at the words in one way while the reader is looking at them in another. While we're on the highway we might take note of those No Overtaking signs. They're all wrong as well, of course."

Percy's forehead wrinkled. "I don't see why . . ."

"Well, what do they really mean?" Charles interrupted. "You know what overtaking means? It's the same thing as overhauling, in the nautical sense. It means catching up with the vehicle (or vessel) in front. What the signs should be saying to you is No Passing."

"Bit awkward for traffic coming the other way," Percy murmured with a twinkle in his eye.

Charles raised an eyebrow. "In what way?" he enquired.

Gene cut in quickly. "OK, let's leave the road and go by rail," he suggested. "Like most of my fellow countrymen I love your exit signs that say Way Out! I always hope that I shall find myself in a disco rather than the street outside.

"And while were on the subject, I've often been somewhat alarmed by British Rail guards announcing over the public address system that This Train Will Terminate at Fenchurch Street. What happens when it gets there? Does it self-destruct?"

"From the look of that particular terminus it does so on a regular basis," Charles said. "But you're right. It should be the service that terminates, not the train. By the way, have you considered the notice beside the emergency handle or chain? It tells you that the Penalty For Improper Use is £100 or whatever."

"What's wrong with that?" I asked.

"Well, it doesn't mean what it says, that's all. If you used the handle improperly it probably wouldn't work, would it? So the real penalty for improper use would be that the train wouldn't stop as desired. The notice should specify the Penalty For Unwarranted Use."

Percy made a small sound in his throat and hastily buried his face in his glass. Charles affected not to hear him.

Gene again came to the rescue. "Some of these railroad stories may be apocryphal," he said, "but I've always liked the one about the little old lady who wanted to cross a station bridge to get to another platform. She came up to the ticket collector in distress and asked, 'How am I to cross the line? The notice on the bridge says that Dogs Must Be Carried. But I'm afraid I don't have a dog!'"

Charles nodded. "Quite so. Of course, public notices don't have to be on placards. Some very small ones come on chemist's bottles. You know the ones. They usually advise: One Tablet To Be Taken Three Times A Day. That's impossible! After all, when you've taken the one tablet the first time it is no longer available for the second and third consumption. The trouble is caused by equating a terminal activity – swallowing a tablet – with a rate of occurrence – three times a day."

Gene bent a look of awed fascination on him. "You're unreal, Charles," he said. "Just what would you put on the bottle if you were a chemist?"

"Oh, I don't know. A logical instruction, at least. Three Tablets A Day, One At A Time would do."

I smiled. "Well, I'm glad we've sorted out public notices," I remarked, "because I've now realised, listening to you, Charles, that they're *all* wrong. I mean, they're not notices put up by the public. They're mostly *authority* notices for general information. Police Notices or Council Notices, say. True public notices are graffiti!"

Noticeable Errors

Percy looked at me. "Don't you start," he said. "I have enough trouble reading notices to pay, like gas bills. Tell you what, though. There's one public notice that has always intrigued me."

We leaned closer. "Yes," he said, "I've always wanted to see one promise fulfilled. It's the notice in the trolley bus that advertises Passengers Alight At Both Ends!"